PRAIRIE FIRE

PRAIRIE FIRE

KAYT C. PECK

SAPPHIRE BOOKS

SALINAS, CALIFORNIA

This and other Sapphire Books titles can be found at
www.sapphirebooks.com

Dedication

To Joe Bob James, a cowboy's cowboy. I never told him he was a hero to me. To Chris Svendsen, the visionary behind Sapphire Books. I learned my lesson. I'll tell her now that she's a hero to me.

Prologue

Judy was a rancher, pure and simple. From the time she drew her first breath, country air gave her lungs the power they needed to cry her proclamation that she was now a living, breathing member of the human race. Her first memory was of sitting in the saddle in front of her mother as they rode, the whole family doing their part in the annual gathering of the yearlings. That memory included her mother's gentle hand, holding her in place. Judy was barely old enough to be out of her crib.

Judy was a rancher; her parents and grandparents had been ranchers. Her great-grandfather and great-great-grandfather had been among those who first gathered the wild Longhorns from the Texas Hill Country, part of the very founders of the modern cattle industry, an industry they followed north from South Texas into the Panhandle where they found their own land and made their ranching tradition.

Like most country kids, she'd tried to leave, but for Judy, it wasn't because she longed to leave for a bigger world. For Judy, it was because she longed to be her true self, a self she believed would never be welcome on the land and among the people in her ranch home, her ranch roots. A woman who loved women… well…the country preacher in their little rural church certainly made clear the sinfulness of homosexuality. College brought Judy her first experiences of the truth she'd secretly known about herself from the time she was thirteen.

A short-lived career as a graphic artist took her to city life, and it was there she found Sandy and the joy of true love. A joy that, in time, she thought she'd have to give up forever. When a car wreck took her parents, Judy had to make a choice – to continue life with Sandy and watch the family ranch sold and parceled out to modern-day hobby ranchers, or to go home to continue the family tradition. Her love for Sandy could not outweigh her love for the land, for the life that was in her blood.

She chose the land. She chose solitude. She chose loneliness, or so she thought, until Kathleen Romero arrived unexpectedly, a woman whose love of writing brought her to a lonely ranch where they both found unexpected gifts in each other and in a shared love for the land. As time passed, it just got better and better.

Chapter One

From Heaven to Hell

The bed felt good, damn good, but not as good as the woman lying beside her. Judy woke slowly, enjoying the little piece of heaven that was now the start of all her days. Two years, it had been. Two years since Kathleen walked into her solitary life, totally unexpected, like a gift from the Universe. Judy snuggled close, spooning beside her lover, burying her face in the vanilla scent of Kathleen's hair.

Chores awaited. Judy knew the horses were probably already snorting in the corrals, waiting for breakfast, and there were chickens to feed and eggs to gather, a new development that Kathleen had insisted they add to their country life. Judy didn't mind the extra work. Fresh eggs were well worth a few minutes work each morning, and Judy had a growing affection for Cogburn, their bantam rooster. The morning ritual of the nose to beak greeting between Cogburn and her dog, Useless, was a joy she had grown to count on as she watched the depth of this non-traditional friendship.

Very soon, Judy would put on her boots, jeans, and worn denim shirt and head outside, but not yet. Now she was warm and comfortable and holding the woman she loved more than she ever thought she could love anyone.

"Ummmmm," Kathleen said.

"You awake?" Judy whispered into Kathleen's hair.

"Reluctantly," Kathleen mumbled into the pillow.

Judy nibbled playfully where Kathleen's neck conjoined with her shoulder.

"Okay, not so reluctantly now," Kathleen said as she rolled over, her arm raised, until, with well-practiced synchronicity, they achieved a final position with Kathleen's arm around Judy and Judy's head resting on Kathleen's shoulder. Judy raised slightly, positioning herself for a gentle and deep kiss. Kathleen put her hand playfully over her mouth.

"I have morning breath," she mumbled behind her hand.

Judy nuzzled at the hand barrier. "I love your morning breath," she said.

The kiss was gentle but deep, as much loving familiarity as passion. Judy finally pulled back, positioning herself half atop and half beside her lover.

"I love you," she whispered into her lover's face.

Kathleen's eyes widened, one eyebrow raising in mild disdain. Judy rolled slightly to the side and put her hand over her own mouth.

"Sorry. Guess it's the onions from last night's enchiladas," she said.

Kathleen laughed softly, and reached to brush a whisper of hair from her lover's face. "I love you too, Judy Proctor, morning breath and all." She nestled her face between Judy's breasts and inhaled deeply. "The rest of you smells absolutely wonderful."

Judy smiled and chuckled, inhaling deeply to enjoy the combined scents of their sleepy bodies. Mid-breath, she stopped, sitting up abruptly.

"I thought you liked my morning breath,"

Kathleen said

"Smell," Judy said harshly.

"What? The onions aren't that bad," Kathleen answered.

"Smell," Judy demanded again.

Kathleen sat up and inhaled deeply. Her face registered surprise and concern. They looked at each other with shared urgency.

"Smoke," they said in unison.

The leisurely morning evaporated. In minutes, they were both in clothes and boots and heading out the front door. Both dogs, Useless and Somegood, crawled from their summer beds beneath the porch, greeting their mistresses, but neither woman took time for the usual pet and scratch behind the ears. Instead, their attention was focused on a wall of smoke not a mile south of their home and ranch headquarters. Prairie fire!

"Call the fire department," Judy yelled as she started for the barn.

"Call 911?" Kathleen asked.

"No, the fire department number posted on the refrigerator. The 911 number doesn't work here," Judy answered, pausing to turn and look at Kathleen.

"It will take them an hour to get here," Kathleen said.

"Call anyway. Then call the Kentons," Judy yelled as she ran toward the barn. The thought of the Kentons gave her more comfort than the distant fire department in the town of Dulson. They were neighbors, friends, and a second family. She felt she could face almost anything with a Kenton by her side. For three generations, the Proctors and the Kentons had watched each other's backs.

"What will we do?" Kathleen yelled.

Judy barely paused, pivoting briefly back toward Kathleen. "Fight it! Shut Somegood and Useless in the house," she said.

At a dead run, Judy half climbed, half jumped over the fence to the horse pasture behind the barn. She ran to the far end and opened the wire gate leading to the far larger cattle pasture behind the house. The horses were agitated in the corrals, troubled by the smoke. She opened the corral gate, and her horse, Jackson, Kathleen's gelding, Dancer, and her late father's horse, Big Tom, thundered past, glad to be free of the corrals.

"Stay free of the fire, boys. That's all the help I can give you," Judy said, her heart twisted in fear for the horses she loved.

Badly winded, Judy forced herself to slow her pace as she headed back to the barn. A broken ankle from a wild run would make her useless as the community gathered to fight the fire. Judy grabbed a stack of gunnysacks from the feed room and a wide scoop shovel from the small metal silo where they stored oats for the horses. Judy knew that the sacks and the shovel had the wide surface area so helpful in beating down the flames of a grass fire. She hoped they'd still work. In her life, she'd fought two prairie fires, both small. As she trotted back to the house where her truck was parked, she looked south to the billows of smoke, knowing exactly where the fire was. It was a field where her father had planted winter wheat for decades. For five years, that field had been part of the federal Crop Reduction Program (CRP), planted back to grass and left untouched. The grass was higher and thicker than any she'd ever seen on her semi-arid prairie. She prayed the methods she knew would work. She thought about the brief thunderstorm she and Kathleen had driven through the night before while coming home from dinner in town. *Lightning*, Judy thought. *Lightning had to have started it.*

Kathleen stood by the truck, holding a shovel from the garden and a gallon milk jug of drinking water.

"Can I use this?" Kathleen asked, holding up the shovel.

"Perfect," Judy answered.

"Fire department is on the way. Julie Kenton said Curley Thomas already picked up Harold, Brad, and Martha, and they're on their way over."

Judy's heart went cold as she looked at her lover. She felt fear like none she'd ever known as she envisioned Kathleen, surrounded by fire.

"Honey, you don't have to go. I mean, it's not…"

"Fuck you. This is my home too," Kathleen answered.

The cold steel Judy saw glinting in Kathleen's eyes made it clear there would be no more argument. Both women were so engrossed in each other and the silent conflict that neither of them noticed the pickup roaring down the county road beside the house until it turned into the yard and slammed to a halt, raising a dense cloud of dust.

"Get in!" Brad Kenton, Judy's best friend since childhood, yelled from the bed of the truck.

Curley Thompson, another neighbor, was driving and Judy could see Brad's parents, Harold and Martha Kenton, riding shotgun and middle inside the cab. Other neighbors would be coming as they saw smoke, but these were the only ones close enough to be of immediate help. Judy and Kathleen threw sacks, shovels, and water jug into the truck bed and climbed inside, barely having time to take a seat before Curley spun around in the circular drive and was back on the county road, heading for the fire. Brad jumped out to open the gates, throwing them aside, leaving them open for the fire trucks. Curley's truck bounced precariously over the rough ground, pushing its way through the thick grass. Judy felt a new fear, concern that the manifold from the truck would ignite even more fires. Curley drove around the fire and directly to its head, just as Judy and her father had done before on the two small fires she'd fought. Then as now, neighbors came together to face a common threat. Both fires were out before the Dulson County fire trucks arrived. She prayed the same would be true this day. Judy, Kathleen, and the Kentons jumped from the truck, grabbing sacks and shovels as they did so. Curley yelled something unintelligible and drove away; Judy assumed he would wait for the fire trucks and lead them through the complex of gates from the main highway to the field.

Like Berserkers, they fought fire. Brad and Harold took sharp shovels, doing the heavy work of chopping out the tufts of grass too dense to be beaten into submission. Judy, Kathleen, and Martha used gunnysacks and shovels to beat at the flames, moving foot by foot to extinguish the dry tender of dense prairie grass. For a time, all went well. They made real progress. Unfortunately, nature can be a real bitch.

Prairie winds are a fact of life. Their caresses on the blades of the ubiquitous windmills made possible settlement of this rich cattle country where surface water is as rare as hen's teeth. Prairie winds bring the rain, pump the water, and make the hot, dry days of summer just a little more bearable. In the 1930s, prairie winds yanked farmers by the scruff of the neck, letting them know the consequences of applying wet land farming methods on the semi-arid prairie. The winds could be friend or foe, depending on many things, especially the foolishness of humanity in thinking it can out guess nature.

The winds changed direction and speed, and the battle turned.

No one said a thing, but they all knew it was time to run for their lives. Half-burned grass where they thought they'd won that battle line suddenly reignited and a wall of flame threatened to swamp them all. Shovels and sacks were dropped, and they ran, coughing at smoke and all taking the same path, around the phalanx of the fire and toward the side where the wall of fire did not extend, into a small break and to relative safety in the black where the fuel was already consumed. No one can understand that moment unless they've been there, in the urgency and confusion of a life and death moment, caring for yourself and yourself alone not because of a choice, but because all that's real in that second is the two feet in one's immediate vicinity and the reflexes that determine whether a person will live or die.

Forty years earlier, Harold Kenton had been star quarterback for the Dulson High School Wolves. His senior year, he was a month away from a college scholarship when they made the play that changed his life. He'd been sacked before, but this Blarneyton Fighting Irish nose-guard was big and as they went down, Harold's knee bent in a way no knee was intended to bend. They carried him off the field that night, ending his football days. Surgery put everything more or less back where it was supposed to be. He'd barely noticed his handicap in the decades following, able to work and ride and do anything a rancher needed to do. He'd barely noticed until making the most important run of his life, a run not from a defensive lineman, but from fire itself. He could see past the smoke and to the safety beyond when that forty-year-old injury said no more and the knee gave way. Harold went down like a ton of bricks. Instinct set in and he crawled to a small area that was more dirt than grass. He curled into a ball, pulling his weathered Stetson tight onto his head, then putting his arms over his face and tucking his hands beneath him. He waited.

Strange thing, the human mind in crisis. As he lay there in those moments that seemed like eternity, all he could do was try to remember the name of that long ago nose-guard. *Damn*, Harold thought. *It's awful not to remember the name of the man who killed you.*

The others coughed and sputtered as they caught their breath in the relative safety of the blackened grass. Martha dropped to her knees and retched from the coughs she could not stop. Brad knelt beside his mother, holding her up by the shoulders. He wiped away his smoke induced tears, streaking even more the soot that covered his face and looked around, assessing the situation.

"Where's Dad?" Brad asked.

Judy and Kathleen joined him, looking around in panic for their missing neighbor. That's when they heard the screams.

"No!" Brad yelled and started to run toward his own demise in the flames. Judy tackled him just a few feet from the fire and Kathleen jumped into the fray, helping her lover hold down the determined son. Brad threw a punch, catching Judy in the right eye, inflicting what would be an awesome shiner and making her see a whole night sky full of stars.

"Brad, stop! You can't help him yet," Martha yelled.

Brad halted his struggle, hearing his mother's words.

Grass fire moves quickly. It seemed like an eternity before the flames passed the spot from which they heard screams then groans. In reality, it was less than a minute. As soon as the fire passed that spot, they were all there, kneeling beside the still curled Harold, horrified at the blackened color of his shirt, even the skin beneath. His Stetson was blackened and smoldering, but still seemed intact. He groaned softly.

"Harold, honey, how are you?" Martha said, kneeling beside her husband.

Harold curled tentatively out of his fetal position, straightening his legs, careful not to roll onto his burnt back. They all knelt in a semi-circle around their burned comrade.

"Troy," he said. "His name was Troy."

"What the hell you talking about, Dad?" Brad demanded.

"That's the name of the man who…well, I guess he didn't kill me," he said, a note of surprise in his voice.

Kathleen looked beyond the tight group, her attention drawn to a flash of light. She spotted the red lights of firetrucks, Curley's pickup leading the rescue caravan.

"Thank God, they're here," Kathleen said. Judy and Brad hooted when they too spotted the welcome site.

Curley pulled his truck near the small group and jumped out of the cab.

"What the hell? Harold, damn it. Harold, you okay?" Curley asked.

Harold groaned and tried to sit up.

"Just lie still, honey," Martha instructed, and Harold obeyed.

"No, Curley old man, I'm not okay, but at least I'm only medium rare instead of well done."

All three fire trucks stopped near the group. Firefighters got out of the trucks. At two of the trucks, firefighters worked some magic at the controls on the side. From one truck, a firefighter, holding a hose and nozzle, took a position in a metal cage in the bed of the truck. On the other, an odd nozzle on the front bumper began to move as though it had a mind of its own. Judy watched in fascination as each truck took a position at the rear of both flanks of the fire and moved slowly forward, spraying a fan of water on the flames, putting the entire fire out, moving from back to front.

The third, smaller truck had a medical emblem on the side. It pulled close to the group of friends and neighbors. A man wearing a white helmet and a woman in a blue helmet exited the truck and pulled medical equipment from a compartment on the side.

"Make room please," the man said as he walked toward Harold.

All but Martha moved aside. She stayed close, holding Harold's relatively unburned hand. The man knelt beside Harold, looking closely at his burned back, not touching.

"Harold Kenton, what the heck you been doing?" the man asked.

Harold began to shiver uncontrollably. "Getting myself charcoaled. Can't you tell?"

"How do, Ted?" Martha said.

"Better than your husband," the man answered.

Once Martha used his name, Judy knew who he was. Ted Rome had been Dulson fire chief for as long as she could remember.

The woman in the blue helmet arrived, carrying two packs of medical equipment, one marked "Burn Kit" in large letters. She wore an orange vest that had a blue EMT emblem over the left front pocket and different gadgets filling almost every pocket. She donned surgical gloves and gently pulled away burned fragments of Harold's shirt.

"What you think, Sally?" the chief asked.

"Call an air ambulance," the EMT answered.

Ted pulled a small electronic box that Judy didn't recognize from off his belt, punching a button to turn it on. He then took the radio from another pouch on his belt. "This is Dulson One to Dispatch. Call air evac and tell them to put a bird in the air."

"Dispatch copies and will call now. What are the coordinates?" came the crackly answer over the radio.

"Have them launch the bird toward Dulson and then standby for coordinates," Ted responded. "Advise air medivac that we have a 50ish male with first, second, and possibly third degree burns to his back."

There was pause of a few moments as Ted stared anxiously at the mysterious electronic device. Judy realized it must be a Global Positioning System (GPS) unit.

"Air ambulance has confirmed message and anticipates being airborne within five minutes," the radio crackled.

"Coordinates for Landing Zone are..." Ted responded, giving a series of numbers that meant nothing to the ranchers surrounding him.

When dispatch repeated and confirmed the coordinates, Ted turned to the paramedic.

"You got this, Sally?" he asked.

"I got it, Chief," she responded.

Ted walked to the parked truck, driving it away to join the other two trucks as they sought out and drowned hot spots in the still smoldering field.

Judy turned her attention from the chief to the paramedic, a woman she vaguely recognized as a teacher in town. She had no idea the woman was also in the fire department. As they all watched, the woman looked more closely at Harold's back, and then gave him a quick examination from head to toe, identifying the knee injury as well as the burns. Then she carefully removed the burned material of Harold's shirt from his back.

"My name's Sally," she said. She looked at Martha. "Are you his wife?"

"Yes, I am."

A whole series of questions followed, about Harold's medical history and medications. As they talked, the woman used a spray bottle from the burn kit to wash his back as best she could in the dusty field, and then placed clean gauze atop the burns, securing the ends on unburned areas using cloth medical tape. Judy was astounded at the level of professionalism. At one point, the woman turned to Brad and described what compartment in the truck he would find a blanket to cover his shivering father. Then she instructed Martha to lie beside the shivering Harold on his relatively unburned front.

"We need to keep him warm," the woman said.

"Aren't you a teacher at Dulson High?" Judy asked.

"Yes," Sally answered.

Kathleen and Judy exchanged glances.

"You mean you're a volunteer firefighter?" Kathleen asked.

Sally rocked back on her heels, pulling an automatic wrist blood pressure cuff from the medical bag. She laughed.

"I'm a volunteer, yes, but I prefer to do the EMS work. Others prefer the fire fighting."

"But...but..." Brad stuttered, "You're so professional."

Sally ignored him, instead focusing on taking Harold's vital signs, writing the results on the surgical glove on her left hand. She pulled a small oxygen bottle from the bag, and fitted the mask on Harold, carefully removing his charred Stetson.

"Looks to me like you should thank your hat for keeping your head safe," Sally observed.

"Nothing like a good Stetson," Harold answered, his voice shaky.

Sally glanced at Brad. "If you're called to do this work, you have to train. Just because we're not paid, it doesn't mean it's not important to do our job right," Sally said.

Judy looked at the middle-aged teacher in front of her, a woman whom she barely noticed before. She looked at her with a whole new eye now.

With a motherly gesture, Sally brushed a piece of charred grass from Harold's face. "When the paramedics get here, they'll start an IV. That should help a lot. I'm afraid I've done all I can do.

"You've…" Brad choked on his words, fighting tears. "You've done a lot."

There was nothing to do but wait. Judy looked around in the relative calm of the moment. She saw Curley, sitting on the tailgate of his pickup, his sweat-stained hat beside him and his head in his hands. His bald head, lacking the once abundant hair that gave him his nickname, was turning red in the sun. Judy walked to him and Kathleen followed.

"You okay, Curley?"

"God damn, I could have killed you all," Curley answered.

"What are you talking about?" Judy asked.

Curley motioned to where the firefighters worked in teams to expose and then extinguish hotspots. "Did you see what they did? They started at the back of the fire and worked forward. If I'd left you all at the back of the fire instead taking you right to the head, Harold wouldn't have got burned."

Judy sat on the tailgate beside him. "Curley, you just did what we've always done. We did the same thing on other fires around, and it worked. Maybe…maybe we just weren't up to a fire like this."

Curley looked at Judy with watery eyes. "Harold's burned because of me."

Kathleen stepped to the older man and hugged him hard. "Curley, don't do this to yourself."

"She's right, Curley. All any of us can do is our best. If you made a mistake, it's one we all made," Judy said.

The distant sound of a helicopter diverted their attention to the sky. Ted Rome jumped into the smaller fire truck and drove back to where the group waited around Harold Kenton. The fire chief parked then exited the truck. They watched as he tightened the chinstrap on his helmet and checked to make sure none of his clothing or equipment was loose before stepping to an open, level area of the field. He checked the wind direction and then, with his back to the wind, walked to the center of the landing area and raised his arms in a V.

"These folks know what they're doing. They wouldn't have made that mistake." Curley suddenly focused on Judy's face. "What happened to your eye?"

"Just hazards of a hard day," Judy answered. Some piece of her normally happy spirit whispered a silent giggle. She found herself wondering if she'd ever have the chance to give Brad a hard time for blacking her eye.

Chapter Two

Trials and Tribulations

There's a joke in Amber, Texas. They say when the Second Coming is here, folks in Amber will have an extra hour because you can't get to Heaven or Hell either one without going through Dallas first. Yes, if anyone wants a direct flight out of Amber, they better be going to Dallas because that's the only choice.

Folks from rural Dulson County, well, they'll have yet another hour and a half to two hours because they have to drive to Amber first.

For Harold Kenton, he found Hell lying in a burnt field just miles from the home that had always been his Heaven. At least he was saved the two-hour drive to Amber for his medical upgrade from Hell to Purgatory. The helicopter shortened that time to thirty-five minutes. Even in a pain-filled stupor, he managed to enjoy his first helicopter flight, especially with the morphine the flight nurse gave him. Within moments of the morphine injection to his IV, Harold began to hope that he actually might live. When he lay huddled, waiting for the fire to reach him, Harold prayed to live. For a time as the fire consumed him, Harold prayed to die. The burns were a pain he never imagined possible.

They let Martha fly shotgun up front with the pilot. Despite the flight nurse's efforts to keep him firmly on his stomach to minimize pain to his burned back, Harold managed to roll partially on his side so he could see his wife.

"Martha honey, ain't this a fine adventure?" Harold said, speaking as loud as he could over the noise of the helicopter, his voice shaky, despite his efforts to hide his pain.

Martha sat turned to face her husband, her hand resting on his right foot, which a thin thermal blanket covered. His clothes and boots had already been cut away and were now in a plastic bag behind the seat Martha occupied. The other foot was inaccessible, hampered by the leg-length splint the nurse used to protect his injured knee.

Martha squeezed his foot gently. She'd watched, anxious but quiet, as the nurse treated her husband. It was such a relief to see his uncontrollable shivering stop and to hear the sigh she knew meant at least some relief from pain.

"Harold Kenton, you just lie still and do what the nurse tells you," Martha said.

"What you seeing up there, Martha girl?" Harold asked.

"What?" she responded.

"Hell woman, we'll be paying for this helicopter ride for the rest of our lives, and I can't see nothing back here. Tell me what you see."

The nurse laughed and placed a gentle hand on Harold's shoulder. "Mr. Kenton," she said. "Patient attitude means a lot in the healing process. I predict you're going to do well."

Martha chuckled, wiping away a tear of relief. "Harold Kenton, you are a handful."

"Why you married me, isn't it?" Harold took a

deep, rattily breath. The morphine numbed the pain, but nothing could eliminate it. Harold wondered how many thousands of nerve endings now throbbed from the burns.

"Talk to me, woman. I want something else to think about," he said.

Martha shifted her position and looked out the window, talking louder because she was no longer facing her husband.

"Well, look there," she said. "We're already over the Canadian River. It would take us an hour to get here driving. Guess the good spring rains helped the whole country. More water than usual in the river, and the pastures look darned green."

"Tell me more," Harold said.

Martha shifted her focus. "Up this high, I can already see the skyline of Amber."

"You mean all two skyscrapers?" Harold said.

Martha gently thumped his foot. "You hush. One of the buildings I can see is University Hospital, and you better be darned glad it's there."

"I am," he said.

The flight nurse shifted position and rearranged the IV bag and other equipment. She gently pushed Harold back onto his stomach. "We need to get ready to land," the nurse said.

In unison, Martha and Harold both whispered, "Thank God," each hoping the other could not see nor hear the extent of their fear.

※ ※ ※ ※

When Judy and Kathleen arrived at the hospital, Brad and his mother were sitting in the ICU waiting room. Both the Kentons were covered in soot from fighting the fire, although they'd used the hospital restrooms to scrub most of the black off of face and hands. Judy pulled a small rolling suitcase. A petite blonde, looking a tad stunned and confused, walked behind her. When the blonde, Brad's young wife, saw her husband, she rushed to him. Brad stood. They held each other for a long time, saying nothing.

Judy blushed, feeling like a voyeur. She cleared her throat and took a seat beside Martha. Kathleen knelt in front of the older woman and held Martha's hand.

"How is he?" Kathleen asked.

"Doctor said it could be worse," Martha explained. "He said Harold was smart, curling in a ball like he did. Just some minor first degree burns to his arms and hands, and his hat, boots, and jeans kept him from anything but a small area of second degree burns on his buttocks. His thin shirt didn't help all. They say there's a mix of second and third degree burns on his back, about twenty percent of his body. He may need some skin grafts."

"They going to keep him here or send him on to the burn center in Lubbock?" Judy asked.

Brad and Julie had finally separated, although she was wrapped around his right arm as they took seats across from the others.

"For now, they'll keep him here," Brad said. "He's stabilizing, and they just want to keep him hydrated and as comfortable as possible for the first twenty-four hours. Doctor said it's not an immediate life threatening situation and that the additional travel would probably do more harm than good."

"Besides," Martha added. "The knee's pretty bad.

Doc told us all the stuff tore loose, but I can't remember the names. When he's well enough from the burns, he's looking at a knee replacement. There's a fine surgeon here who specializes in knee replacements."

"Damn! Poor Harold," Judy said.

"Have you been in to see him?" Kathleen asked.

"Every couple of hours they let two go in to see him in ICU," Brad answered. "He's mostly sleeping. Good drugs, I guess, and when he is awake he's pretty loopy."

"I haven't seen him this toasted since before you were born, son," Martha said.

Brad looked at his mother, slack-jawed. "Dad got drunk?"

Martha chuckled, a soft look in her eye, a look of a fond memory. "When we were engaged and in college, one summer Harold decided he was going to be a rodeo bronc rider, but he was a country boy hanging with experienced rodeo circuit riders. Oh, he'd had a beer or two before, but it was his first introduction to whiskey. When they went up to Dalhart for the XIT Rodeo and Reunion, his buddy Carlton called me and said I better come get him. By the time I got there, Harold was stripped down to his jockey shorts, Stetson and boots, standing on the tailgate of a truck and singing *San Antonio Rose* at the top of his lungs. I told him he better get down and come home. He said that he was just fine. That was right before he passed out. Luckily, he fell toward Carlton and me. We kept him from going face first into the gravel."

Brad, Judy, and Kathleen all three stared at Martha with opened mouths, too shocked to speak. Julie struggled to stifle a giggle.

"Like father like son," she said softly.

Brad blushed four shades of purple, and Julie's giggle turned into a full-fledged laugh. Like a ripple, Judy joined her with Kathleen and Martha soon following. All the fear and pain of the day eased as they laughed. In the end, even Brad joined in the cacophony, all of them laughing until the tears flowed and Brad got a case of the hiccups.

As she struggled to contain the dwindling giggles, Judy thought, *it's true. There is relief in comedy*.

"Now, none of you all can ever let Harold know I told you," Martha said. "He was so embarrassed that he never competed in another rodeo. Took me two years to get him to even go to see a rodeo and that was only after he grew a mustache and changed his hat style, hoping no one would recognize him."

Brad let out the deep breath he'd been holding to stop the hiccups. "Everything okay at home?" he asked, looking toward Judy.

"All the stock is fed at both our places, and Curley said he'd check on 'em in the morning." Judy pointed at the suitcase beside her. "We packed a few things for all three of you. This is for Harold. The bags for you two are out in your car."

"Before I forget, can I have my car keys back?" Kathleen asked Brad.

After the helicopter left, Curley drove them to Judy and Kathleen's place. The two women gave Brad every bit of cash they had, along with Kathleen's car keys. They told him to go be with his parents at the hospital, and they would follow.

"Harold's not going to need many clothes here," Martha said.

"We packed a pair of sweat pants and a soft shirt for his trip home," Julie said. "Didn't figure he'd be up to wearing jeans for a while, but we remembered his razor and toothbrush and all that."

"Brought the knitting you were working on and some of the books on your nightstand, Martha," Kathleen said.

Martha smiled softly and touched the side of Kathleen's face. "You know, for never giving birth to a daughter, I sure got three sweet ones," she said, smiling at all three of the younger women.

A nurse walked into the waiting room, a scowl on her face. "Everything all right in here? I heard a terrible row from the hallway."

Brad gave a giggle. Judy pointed a finger at him. "Now stop that before you get the hiccups again."

"We're fine, honey. We just...well...I told a funny story," Martha said

The nurse's scowl eased slightly. "Looks like you've had more family arrive."

"Yes." Martha motioned toward Julie. "This is my daughter-in-law, and this," She indicated Judy, "is my daughter of the heart and this," Martha hesitated briefly, thinking, as she looked at Kathleen, "is my other daughter-in-law."

"But, you only have the one son?" the nurse asked.

"Yes ma'am," Martha answered, a glint of defiance in her eyes.

The nurse looked around the circle of family, confused. Judy reached for Kathleen's hand, gently intertwining her fingers with Kathleen's. The nurse's face transformed from confusion to realization to surprise and then amusement.

"Oh," she said. The one word said it all. "Well, just don't forget there's only two at time during the visiting sessions."

"We won't," Martha answered.

The nurse left, and Judy turned to Martha. "When you get time, you might want to give Curley a call," she said.

"Why's that?" Martha responded.

"He blames himself for Harold getting burned."

"Bless that dear soul. It was a fire. Sometimes fire wins."

Kathleen continued to hold Judy's hand, and leaned close to her lover as she joined the conversation. "Curley kept talking about how the trained firefighters started from the back of the fire, going up each side. He thinks if he hadn't dropped us off at the front of the fire, Harold would be just fine."

"Even if he's right, he only did what we've always done at a grass fire. This one was just bigger and hotter than any I've ever seen," Martha said.

There was a silence. Judy stared at the toes of her boots. "It's the CRP grass and the wet spring. I pray we don't see any more fires."

Another nurse entered the room. She had a sweet face, an attractive sixty-something woman. She paused, hesitantly, looking at the family group, smiling directly toward Judy and Kathleen.

"Are you all the Kentons?" The nurse asked.

"Yes ma'am," Martha answered.

"As I was getting off shift, Nurse Johnson suggested I might want to come meet you." The nurse walked toward them, looking quizzically at Judy. "You look rather familiar," the nurse said. "Maybe you know my partner, Tandy."

Judy stood and shook the nurse's hand. "The Tandy who owns the Pink Triangle? Why, everyone knows Tandy."

"I don't," Brad said.

Judy kicked his boot and glared at him. "You run in a different crowd," she said.

Kathleen stood and smiled warmly at the nurse. "Judy took me there once, before I'd decided to move down here permanently. Nice place."

"What's the Pink Triangle?" Martha asked.

Judy and Kathleen shared glances that clearly said, "How do we explain this?"

"Well, Martha, it's a good place to go dancing," Judy answered.

"That sounds nice for you young people. Maybe you should take Brad and Julie sometime."

"Uhhhh," Judy answered.

Brad looked at his best friend with a sly grin. "It might be kinda interesting."

Judy kicked him again.

The nurse introduced herself as Sharon Smith and Judy made the circle of introductions for herself, Kathleen, and the Kentons. Martha leaned close to whisper in Kathleen's ear as Judy and Sharon conversed.

"This Pink Triangle," Martha said in a hushed tone. "Is it one of them gay bars?"

Kathleen laughed and nodded "yes."

"They got 'em in Amber?" Martha asked, speaking a little louder than intended.

Conversation stopped and they all looked at the older woman. Martha blushed.

"Well, I guess we never get too old to learn something new," she said.

A ripple of laughter waved its way through the group.

Sharon looked directly at Judy and Kathleen.

"I know you all have a lot to deal with right now, but Mr. Kenton mainly needs rest and drugs. If you two are interested, we're having our weekly meeting of the Ladies' Room discussion group this evening at seven in the upstairs room of the Pink Triangle."

"Ladies' Room? I saw one of them down the hall," Brad said, a wicked smile on his face.

This time Judy didn't bother with kicking his boot. She went directly for the shin.

"Ouch!" Brad said. "That hurt."

"Good," Judy responded.

"He your brother?" Sharon asked.

"Sort of," Judy answered.

"We claim him, even on his bad days," Kathleen added.

Sharon gave Brad her best and most terrifying nurse's glare. "Better you than me," she said.

Chapter Three

The Ladies' Room

They pulled the car into a space at the back of the Pink Triangle, just where Sharon Smith told them to park. They were late. Judy and Kathleen half-forced Martha to go with them to the hospital cafeteria for dinner while Brad and Julie stayed in the ICU waiting room. Her son promised to call Martha's cell phone if there was any news or changes. At first, all three women picked at their food. After a couple of bites, physical need overshadowed appetite suppression from emotional trauma. They ate like the ranch hands they were, hunger ceasing all conversation as food went from plate to belly. Judy couldn't decide if the hospital food was that good or if they were just that hungry. Only then did she remember there had been no breakfast, and lunch had been a can of mixed nuts and sodas Kathleen and Julie bought at the gas station while Judy filled the car with gas.

The hospital volunteer at the information desk informed them that the Comfort Inn across the road had a special price for patients' families and gave them coupons for the rooms. After checking into two rooms, one for Judy and Kathleen and another for the three Kentons, the three women grabbed quick showers and a change of clothes. When Judy and Kathleen stepped out of their room, they noticed that Brad's car had moved from the space where Martha had parked it when they first arrived. Judy knocked at the door to the Kentons' room. Brad answered the door, wearing the bathrobe his wife had packed for him and toweling still wet hair.

"Where's Martha?" Judy asked.

"She's at the hospital with Julie," Brad answered. "She told me to tell you two to go on to this Ladies' Room thing tonight. We're fine, and we want stories tomorrow. Mama's downright curious."

"And you aren't?" Judy asked.

Brad grinned. "Well, maybe a little."

They finally arrived at the Pink Triangle at seven fifteen.

"I hate being late," Kathleen said.

"Don't worry. I'm sure they're on gay standard time," Judy responded. She looked at the wooden steps leading up to the second floor room. "All the years I've been coming to the Pink Triangle, I never even noticed that room existed."

They could see lights in the windows, and as they stood looking toward the room, they heard a burst of laughter.

"I wonder if it's a potluck," Kathleen said.

"If it is, tonight we'll bring more pot than luck," Judy said. "They'll understand."

Kathleen looked at her lover with a sly smile. "You brought pot?" It was common knowledge that Judy was a marijuana virgin.

Judy blushed. She swatted Kathleen lovingly on the ass. "Let's go inside."

The stairs creaked some as they ascended toward this mysterious Ladies' Room. Judy noticed new wood on a couple of the steps, obviously recent repairs. The door at the top of the stairs opened and a woman with short brown hair wearing a leather bomber jacket smiled a greeting.

"Welcome," the woman said. "These creaky stairs are better than a door bell."

"We rely on Useless and Somegood at home," Judy answered.

"Useless and Somegood?" the woman asked.

"Our ranch dogs," Kathleen answered.

The woman stood to the side, ushering them into the room. "I like that. My dog's name is Nearly."

"Nearly?" Judy asked.

"Nearly Human is the full name," the woman responded. "Welcome, I'm April Sims. I'm sort of the coordinator for The Ladies' Room." She offered her hand, and Judy shook it firmly. Judy was pretty sure she'd just found her new best friend.

The room was full. Women sat in a huge circle of chairs and couches. Some of the younger women along with a couple of children sat on the floor toward the center of the circle. One little girl, around five years old, happily played with a pair of Barbies. She was in the middle of changing outfits from beachwear to evening attire. A young woman with spikey short hair and wearing a softball jersey sat beside the child, helping her play but looking out-of-place holding a miniature evening gown.

Judy looked around, but it was almost too much to take in at once. Conversation ceased as all eyes focused on the new arrivals.

"Well, don't I feel like a Guinea in the hen house?" Judy said.

A wave of laughter broke the group silence. Women started to shuffle seats, making room for the new arrivals. April brought two folding chairs to the circle and placed them in space made open by the group.

"Welcome," said a handsome Latina. "Come, sit beside me," she said, indicating the chairs April had just placed; a third empty chair was on her other side.

"This is my partner, Sophia," April said, introducing the Latina.

Kathleen dropped to the chair beside Sophia, placing a hand on the woman's arm. "Please forgive my Guinea-bird here." Kathleen smiled and tilted her head toward Judy. "She tends to say what's on her mind."

Sophia hugged Kathleen. "Don't I understand? I have one of those too."

Judy dropped to a seat in the proffered chair. "Sorry we're late. We've been at the hospital with a friend."

"Glad you came," Sharon Smith said from a seat on the other side of the room.

"Thank you for inviting us," Kathleen responded.

Judy saw Tandy, owner of the Pink Triangle, sitting beside Sharon. They exchanged a quiet wave hello.

"I told Kathleen it would be fine. I was sure you'd be on gay standard time," Judy added.

The ball player reluctantly playing Barbies spoke. "April's got us trained. Discussion starts at seven."

"You make me sound like a task master," April said. A wave of playful agreement rippled through the room. April blushed but smiled. "Okay, maybe a little bit, but damn, people have things to say."

"Speaking of which," a woman said, a hint of reprimand in her voice. "As I was saying, I really want this group's advice."

Judy looked at the speaker and was confused. The woman obviously bought top line designer clothing, and she sported perfect fingernails painted a lovely purple to match her outfit. Still, the bow in her hair made Judy's gaydar peg out at a total zero.

"I don't understand why my husband insists on sitting around the house in his underwear. Why, I caught the neighbor looking in the living-room window last weekend, and she looked way too pleased at what she saw."

Kathleen leaned to whisper to Sophia. "Did she say husband?"

Sophia raised a finger and spoke to the group. "If I may interrupt for a minute, Sara Jean. We may need to explain to our newcomers that this is a group open to any woman – as long as she is open minded – lesbian or straight."

"My goodness, yes," Sara Jean said. She looked directly at Kathleen. "They advertised this as a Lambda meeting, and I showed up thinking it was a chapter of my college sorority. Had so much fun, I kept coming back, and I swear these women help me understand men better than any group I've ever known."

Judy sat with her mouth open, staring at the woman. Kathleen gently pushed at Judy's jaw, closing the open mouth.

"Anyway, what do you think?" Sara Jean asked the group.

"My husband does the same thing," said the woman sitting on the couch behind the little girl playing dolls. "When they say 'home is their castle,' they mean they want to be comfortable and…well… just be a guy."

Judy's mouth dropped open again. The woman sitting beside the mother on the couch stifled a giggle and looked at Judy. "Hi, I'm Mo." She jerked her thumb toward the woman beside her. "She's my sister. She comes to help keep me in line," the woman said.

"Well, what do I do?" Sara Jean asked. "How do I get him to stop?"

"You don't," Judy said. All eyes turned to her. "Well, you don't. Oh, if you nag long enough, you might stop it for a while, but he's not going to change. Not 'cause of nagging, anyway."

"She knows of what she speaks," Kathleen added. She leaned an elbow on her knee, placed her chin on her hand, and looked intently at her lover. "She can be very…male, sometimes."

Judy directed a cheesy grin at Kathleen, and the group laughed.

"She's right," said another woman dressed in the same softball jersey as the young woman sitting on the floor. "He'll listen. He may nod agreement, but he won't change unless he wants to for his own reasons."

"So what do I do?" Sara Jean asked, a note of desperation in her voice.

"Close the shades," April said.

"What?" Sara Jean asked.

"When he's watching TV in his BVDs, close the shades," Mo added.

"And you might want to have a little talk with your neighbor," Mo's sister said.

Sara Jean's eyes narrowed angrily. "I like that idea."

"Does he like football?" April asked.

Sara Jean looked at her mockingly. "Well, duh. He is a guy, and he was the team captain in high school."

"What's his favorite team?" April continued.

"The Cowboys, of course."

"Go buy him a nice soft set of lounging pajamas with a Cowboys' logo."

Mo laughed and slapped her knee. "That's brilliant."

Sophia tilted her head to one side, looking at April, and spoke softly, almost to herself. "Cowboy lounging pajamas…good idea."

April cleared her throat. "Or Broncos. Broncos might be better for some…guys."

The group laughed.

"Luckily, our nearest neighbors are five miles away," Kathleen said.

"Unless you count cattle and horses," Judy said.

"Well, I seem to have an old cow living next to me," Sara Jean added. There was more laughter.

"Where do you live?" Tandy asked Judy from across the room.

"On a ranch on the far side of Dulson County," Judy answered.

"You had a grass fire up there today, didn't you?" one woman asked. "I saw it on the news. Someone got hurt."

"That's why we're here," Kathleen explained. "He was our dear friend and neighbor, Harold Kenton. We're here to support him and his family."

"How is he?" Sharon Smith asked.

Judy took a deep breath. For a moment, she'd forgotten the worry and fear for the man who was like a father to her. "Second and third degree burns on twenty percent of his body, but he's stable. Pretty drugged up, though. He'll have to have knee surgery. That's how he got burned. Knee gave out and he couldn't run from the fire."

"My goodness. He'll be in the hospital for some time," Sharon observed.

"I live over near the hospital," Mo said. "You need a place to stay?"

"We got a room at the Comfort Inn. We have to get back to the ranch tomorrow. We'll be looking after both places while the family is here," Judy said. She paused, thinking. "Would you…would you mind if we gave your number to Martha, Harold's wife? I know her. She'll stay right here in Amber until Harold's able to go home. She may need options."

"Once he's in a regular room, they'll let her stay with him," Sharon said. "But that may be awhile."

"You bet," Mo responded. "Would she mind staying in a lesbian house?"

"She's fine with Kathleen and me," Judy said. "But it did take some getting used to for her."

Kathleen laughed. "You should have heard how shocked she was to learn that Amber has a gay bar."

"I was too," Sara Jean said. "Told John, my husband, and he wants to come here dancing, but I think he secretly wants to watch you women."

Tandy laughed. "Bring him," she said. "We'll get one of the fellas to make a pass at him, and he'll never come back."

The group laughed, especially Mo. "Let us know what night," she said. "So we can watch the show."

"I will. I most certainly will," Sara Jean answered.

Before the evening was over, everyone had their chance to talk, although at eight o'clock, they took a break and hit the potluck table like vultures on a carcass. When Judy and Kathleen protested they hadn't brought food, various women forced paper plates into their hands and advised on which dishes were the best. Most recommendations ended with a confession that the one the advisor had brought was best. Between eating the meal they'd shared with Martha and taking small portions of all dishes, Judy and Kathleen were seriously stuffed by the time the group disbanded and they headed down the stairs toward their car; their pockets held scraps of paper with various names and phone numbers.

They were saying goodbye to new friends in the parking lot when Kathleen's cell phone rang. Judy held her breath, fearing bad news about Harold. She sighed in relief when she heard Kathleen speak.

"Pookie, how are you?" Kathleen walked to a quieter spot behind the stairs. Judy was relieved. She knew of Pookie, one of the young lesbians Kathleen had mentored back Colorado. Mo was just finishing giving Judy her recipe for red beans and rice when Kathleen returned, a worried crease between her eyes.

"Everything okay?" Judy asked.

"When it rains, it pours," Kathleen answered.

"What's wrong?"

"Let's talk about it in the car," Kathleen said.

Judy said nothing, but watched her lover's face closely as they got in the car, Judy in the driver's seat. "Now tell me," Judy said.

Kathleen took a deep breath. "Do you remember Pookie? You met her when we went up to get the last of my stuff in Colorado Springs."

"Forget Pookie? Not likely. First time I ever really got to know someone with a pierced tongue and eyebrow."

"That's my Pookie. Well, her step-father kicked her out of the house."

"Geeze, because she's gay?"

"Gay and distinctly non-traditional. She's graduated from high school, and he wants her to go to beautician school. She wants to work on her art. She's staying on the couch at a friend's house for a couple of days, but then she has nowhere to go."

"She's got talent, I'll give you that, but I might back the step-father on some things," Judy said.

Kathleen's lips compressed into a thin line. "Judy, she's like a daughter to me."

Judy paused, her hand on the keys in the ignition switch. She thought for a moment, looking out the windshield, seeing nothing. To her credit, it was only a moment.

"If she's family to you, she's family to me," Judy said, starting the car. "We'll get her a bus ticket tomorrow."

Tears of gratitude gave an extra sheen to Kathleen's eyes. Judy wondered what would have happened if the girl had not been welcomed. She knew her lover, the size of her heart, and the extent of her integrity. Judy didn't want to think what might have happened had the conversation gone differently.

Pookie, Judy thought, remembering the tiny girl with all black clothes and purple hair. *Oh Lord, what's going to happen now?*

Chapter Four

Seeds of an Idea

The gate squeaked loudly as Judy opened the back of the aging stock trailer. Jackson, her bald-faced gelding, backed out confidently, Judy catching the reins draped around his neck as he stepped free. She led him away from the trailer and Brad stepped inside, opening the gate midway up the trailer to release his own bay horse. Horses and riders all moved with a choreography born of familiarity. They knew why they were there and what job needed doing. Judy breathed in the familiar smells of horse dung and dust and smiled. Days like this were as close as she expected to come to Heaven on this side of life. Sometimes she looked forward to crossing that divide and riding once again at her father's side.

Judy tightened the front cinch on her saddle, stepped into the stirrup, and pulled herself easily into the saddle, having to lift her leg just a bit higher than normal to clear full saddlebags. They held bottles of medicine, syringes, a fencing tool, and fence staples, all things a cowhand might need while out making rounds checking the health and well-being of bovines, windmills, and aging barbed-wire fence. Over two miles of the north boundary fence on the Proctor ranch were built in the 1880s, part of the original XIT Ranch. She patched, mended, and nursed that fence, striving to protect an important piece of history.

She sat lightly in the saddle as she watched Brad adjust his own saddle then step aboard his bay gelding. It felt good to be out again. In the month Harold had been in the hospital, Judy and Kathleen tried to keep up the maintenance on both ranches, with occasional help from Curley, but it was a relief to have her life-long friend and consistent work companion back for a few days. Kathleen was a better hand than Judy ever would have dreamed when she first met the writer. The designer jeans and fancy blouses Kathleen wore at their first meeting had no hint of her potential to love ranching life. Kathleen took to ranching like a fish to water, something Judy better understood as she met her family, their roots deeply embedded in the centuries old Hispanic families of northern New Mexico. Kathleen had the land in her genes and her heart. She only needed the opportunity to give it life. Wranglers and chambray shirts had replaced the designer jeans and fancy blouses, except for special occasions. Whether she wore designer jeans or Wranglers didn't matter; Kathleen's beauty still robbed Judy of her very breath.

"Talked with your momma this morning?" Judy asked.

"Sure did."

"How's your dad?"

"Cranky as a cow right before calving," Brad answered.

"Good. Glad to hear it. Means he's getting better."

"Doctors are surprised how fast he's healing. That one skin graft they had to do took just fine. Dr. Thompson announced before I left that they'd do the knee surgery next week. They think he may be ready to come home in a couple of weeks."

"That's good news indeed."

"Sure was nice of Kathleen to offer to go stay with Momma for a while so Julie and I could come home," Brad said. "Nice too of your friends there to rent Momma a room. Cheaper and a lot more comfortable than a hotel."

They rode slowly through the herd of Angus-Hereford cross stocker calves, looking for signs of anything sick or injured. Both riders had catch-ropes tied to their saddle-horns in case a steer needed to be roped, thrown, and "doctored." These calves had settled in nicely, past the threat of the "shipping sickness" that could be so devastating when a new batch arrived. It was stress, pure and simple, Judy knew. Being gathered, packed in a truck, and dumped in a whole new place was bound to make a few sick from pure old trauma. Judy always preferred to raise their own calves from birth to feeder weight, even keeping a select batch to sell special for the individual meat-packers specializing in grass-fed beef. Still, stockers were a fact of life for a viable, modern ranch. It took less grass and land than maintaining enough cow/calf pairs to use the land efficiently but sustainably. Judy pulled her thoughts back to the conversation at hand.

"It wasn't just being nice," Judy responded. "We got heifers about to calve both places. Kathleen would rather sit in a hospital waiting room than be assistant obstetrician to a bunch of heifers."

Brad scrunched up his face, thinking. "It's kind of a toss-up to me, but I will say it sure feels good to be breathing fresh air for a while."

There hadn't been a sign of a sick calf or cow all day, even as they checked the last pasture. For Judy, it had just been a pleasant day in the company of an old friend, more a brother than a friend. They rode in silence for some time, each knowing without being told it was their job to lay eyes on every animal as they rode past, looking for any sign of distress.

"You know, Judy girl, I been doing a lot of thinking, sitting around that hospital," Brad said.

"You? Thinking? Better call Debbie at the newspaper. This could be a front-page story."

"Hardy har har," Brad answered. "I'm being serious."

The smile disappeared from Judy's face. "What you thinking?"

"Remember the day of the fire?"

Judy looked at Brad in surprise. "Remember the day of the fire? How the hell could I forget?"

"I guess I mean do you remember how the firefighters from town worked together?"

"Sure do. We're damn lucky to have them around here. Not only the fire, I couldn't believe how well they took care of your dad and called in that helicopter."

Brad turned in the saddle to look at his companion. "Lucky to have 'em, but not lucky that it takes nearly an hour for them to get here."

"They do their best, Brad. It's just a long way from town."

"I'm not complaining, but I been thinking."

"Now there you go again."

"Hush up," Brad responded, losing patience. "Judy, did you know the chief and assistant chief are the only paid firefighters?"

"No, I didn't."

"I called the station a couple of times. Mom wanted an address to send a thank you card, and Chief Rome and I got to visiting. Most of the firefighters are volunteers, and there are other volunteer companies around the county."

Judy thought a moment. "I never thought about it much, but I have noticed the fire station by the grain elevator at Conlen."

"Judy, let's do it here."

The novelty of the thought made her speechless for a moment. "You mean start a fire company?"

"Yeah, why not?"

"But you're talking about actually becoming firefighters."

"That's exactly what I'm talking about. If there's a fire out here, we're going to do it anyway. Why not get trained and have the equipment to do it right?"

Judy thought for several minutes, and they rode in silence. After a while, she looked at the position of the sun and the healthy cattle they had nearly finished checking.

"Brad, if we hurry up a bit, we could get the horses unloaded and fed, and the trailer unhitched in time to get to town. I'd like to visit some with Chief Rome myself, see what he thinks."

Brad wheeled his horse around, back the direction of the trailer. "These cattle are fine. Let's get moving," Brad said. "Besides, I wouldn't mind a store-bought steak and some cobbler for dinner. We can pick up Julie at the house."

They were both old enough to know better than to have a horse race back to the trailer. They were old enough to know better, but they did it anyway. Brad won, but then, he had a head start.

Kayt C. Peck

Chapter Five

Pookie Time

A bus is a bus is a bus. Upholstery colors may change, and the wear of seats occupied by a thousand travelers will vary depending on whether the bus just rolled off the assembly line or is a veteran of black-topped highways on the outside and human drama on the inside. There was always the same acrid smell of diesel and the pungent odor of urine that could never be eliminated, no matter how conscientious the cleaning, especially if one took a seat too near the claustrophobic lavatory. Pookie remembered that smell and chose a seat near the front, wondering as she did if they somehow added urine odor at the factory. The only buses she'd ever known without that smell were the sparse and Spartan yellow school buses she'd rode on field trips. No lavatory, no urine odor.

Pookie took a window seat when she first got on at the Greyhound station in Colorado Springs. Mr. Schindler, the father of her best friend - Bobby, the sweet little gay boy - had dropped something in her jacket pocket as she hugged him goodbye. It wasn't until she was on the bus that she pulled out the $20 bill. His hug was brief and an odd combination of gruff and warm. Mrs. Schindler had held her for a long time, not even trying to hide the tears in her eyes. Bobby...oh goodness, Bobby. He had wailed so loudly as he hugged his dearest friend that even Pookie, who didn't much give a fuck what anyone thought, was embarrassed.

Tears threatened to overfill Pookie's eyes as she looked at the money. The Schindlers couldn't afford a gift to their wayward guest. She had been grateful enough for the bed on their living-room couch when her stepfather had pushed her out of the house, not even giving her time to pack a bag. As a janitor at an elementary school, Mr. Schindler didn't make much, and Mrs. Schindler only had part-time work cleaning rooms at a second-rate motel, but what they had, they invested where they knew it was important, their kids. In the case of Pookie, it was their kids and their kids' friend. Pookie had been an honorary member of the family ever since the seventh grade, when she'd confronted bullies as they pantsed delicate little Bobby in the school courtyard beside the gym. Both Pookie and Bobby sported black eyes before the encounter was over, but tiny Pookie made sure each of the two bullies had their own blackened eyes to explain to parents. The principal suspended all four kids for three days, and Mrs. Schindler met with the principal and took them home. It was still just Pookie and her mom then – pre-stepfather, and her mom's boss (Pookie's future stepfather) wouldn't let her leave work when the principal called. When Mrs. Schindler learned that Pookie would be home alone, she took the girl to their house instead. As soon as they arrived, Pookie and Bobby went to his room to listen to his new CD of the *Wicked* soundtrack. Pookie didn't hear the telephone conversation between her mom and Mrs. Schindler, arranging for Pookie to stay with the Schindlers during the suspension. For three glorious days, Pookie had been a member of a real family. She'd learned to change diapers while helping Mrs. Schindler with Elaine, the ten-month-old surprise package now totally spoiled by her two older siblings and now a third, honorary sibling. She'd sat at the table participating in noisy conversations where she was amazed how everyone could talk at once and still know exactly what all said. It was Heaven. It was the happiest she had been since her father died two years earlier.

Pookie was her father's daughter. She learned from him that the only boundaries in life were the ones you created for yourself. With his own graphic design business, Michael Thompson led a busy but flexible life. He was the driving force behind any project at his company, but he hired good people and they did much of the work so that he had time to indulge a daughter who, at a very early age, showed his same passion and talent for visual arts. She had her own corner in his studio at their house. She began with her own finger-painting easel when she was a toddler and grew to her own drawing table and computer with graphics software by the time she was ten. Her mom was something of an outsider to the adventures and visions of her husband and daughter, but she was content. Her mother's ability to be happy with a house to keep and meals to cook would mystify Pookie later in life. As a small child, she was unconsciously comfortable with just knowing her mother was there whenever she needed her; it was almost like a perfect appliance for a comfortable home.

Adventures they did share. Pookie and her dad hiked the rugged Rockies. When Pookie wanted a pony, she got it, and her dad bought a horse; both animals boarded at a dude ranch not far from Colorado Springs. Almost every weekend of the summer, they rode, and her father joined in like another playmate as they pretended to ride from imaginary town to imaginary town, a couple of saddle-tramps looking for adventure and opportunity to right wrongs in the Old West. Joanne Thompson stayed at home or remained in the lodge at the ranch, reading her latest romance novel while father and daughter built a whole new world in their shared imagination. At home, not only did Michael encourage her art, but they also created together. Pookie sold her first painting at the age of six. It was a five-foot by seven-foot abstract landscape she and her father created together with Pookie working low and Michael working high. The two strategized together on how to make the two works meet in the middle. It was then she learned to be herself, for there would always be a way to fit in the big picture.

Then Michael died…a senseless car wreck at an intersection he'd driven a million times. It just took one time and one truck driver who didn't see the stoplight.

Life changed. Pookie's mom tried to take over the business, but she had neither the personality nor the talent. The artists, so successful under Michael's leadership, were nearly useless at the actual business. When Michael's primary competitor offered to buy, Joanne sold the business for nearly nothing along with a promise of a job as office manager. She became at work what she'd been at home, the perfect and always reliable appliance, and she was content.

Pookie was not.

Grief consumed her. Even after her father's funeral, the child insisted for months that he'd be coming home. She was furious when they moved to a smaller house, one her mother could afford, not because she didn't like the new house but because she was afraid her father wouldn't know where to find them. For a long time, it settled into a steady anger, one she directed at righting wrongs just as she and her father had done riding from imaginary town to imaginary town. That's how she found her best friend, Bobby. That's how she found the "clique" of artistic punks who dressed in black and knew tattoo artists and piercing studios that turned a blind eye if a parental consent form didn't look exactly "right." It was also among the punks that she acknowledged and put into practice her natural inclination to love girls and the support available for gay teens through the high school's Gay/Straight Alliance (GSA). One adult volunteer in particular, Kathleen Romero, saw and understood Pookie in a way the girl had only known with her father. Kathleen's passion was words and Pookie's were paint and clay, but Kathleen understood the need to create, to see what others could not and express that vision.

Between the Schindlers, Kathleen, her punk compatriots, and a loving but clueless mother, Pookie finally found a hint of happiness in her now fatherless life. Then, her father's nemesis, the rival who bought the business, decided he wanted more.

As stepfathers went, he wasn't that bad. Mainly, he ignored her, which was fine with Pookie. She was damn good at ignoring him back. That was until her art drew the attention of a gallery owner who worked with the GSA, before she won a full art scholarship to Colorado University in Boulder.

Jealousy is such a nasty beast. The stepfather could own the business, even possess his competitor's wife, but the man would never achieve Michael Thompson's level of talent. He sure as hell wasn't going to live in the shadow of Michael's daughter.

Beauty school at the community college was the stepfather's plan for Pookie, that or just a job. In the month before high school graduation, Pookie would come home to find newspaper classified pages lying on her drawing board with advertisements circled – the ones for fast food restaurants and grocery clerks.

The writing was on the wall, but even Pookie was shocked when it came just two days after graduation. Joanne cried as her new husband pushed her daughter out of the house, but she didn't stop him. Behind his back, the woman mouthed the Schindlers' name, and Pookie nodded understanding.

Now, just four days later, she was on a bus heading to a new life, one she couldn't even imagine. She had a rolling duffle—containing more art supplies than clothes—stashed in the belly of the bus and a backpack in the rack above her seat…all that remained of her former life. She wouldn't have that if Mr. Schindler hadn't gone with her back to her mother's home. The stepfather remained mute, stepping away from the far larger Mr. Schindler, as Pookie and her mother went to Pookie's room and packed what they could in a short time.

"He'll get over this," her mother said. "You can come back."

I doubt that, Pookie thought as she hugged her mother, the woman who had always cared for Pookie tenderly even if she never understood the girl. In an odd way, the realization of how little she would miss her mother, a woman who had always been a stranger to her, saddened Pookie more deeply.

As the miles slipped under the wheels of the bus, Pookie slept, dreaming of riding from imaginary town to imaginary town. She awoke once with an epiphany.

I'm going to a ranch, she thought. *A ranch, just like Dad and I dreamed back when we rode our horses together.*

❧❧❧❧

Judy picked at the congealed gravy from what was left of her chicken fried steak and mash potatoes. True, the Cowboy Café substituted as the local bus station, but it was still known for the quality of its chicken fried steak. Judy barely tasted it as she chewed, her mind on other things.

"My, that's certainly appetizing," Kathleen said from across the booth, her eyes on the mess Judy was making of the remains on her plate.

Judy pushed the plate to the side, took a drink from her nearly empty iced tea glass, shaking a small chunk of ice into her mouth as she did so. She crunched nervously on the ice.

"I've never seen you like this before," Kathleen said.

"Don't ever think I've felt like this before," Judy answered.

"You weren't even this nervous the first time we met."

"Well, this Pookie girl…she means a lot to you. What if she doesn't like the ranch or me? I mean, Lordie, how many cowgirls do you know with a pierced eyebrow?"

"And when we went up to Colorado Springs, you were the only one at the GSA meeting in cowboy boots, but you got along fine," Kathleen countered.

"Yeah, I reckon," Judy said, still fidgeting in her

seat.

"Say it," Kathleen said.

"Say what?"

"Say what else is on your mind."

Judy cleared her throat and took a deep breath. "What…what if I don't like her?"

Kathleen blushed. Judy's pulse quickened as she saw the signs of anger.

"Don't you dare go all conservative on me," Kathleen said. "You give Pookie half a chance, and you'll love her as much as I do."

Judy fidgeted in her seat. "I guess I've just never really known someone who wore black lipstick before. I always managed to sidle away from them when I saw them at the bar in Amber."

"Before you met me?"

"Of course before I met you." Judy gave a smile that was more of a grimace than a smile. "Am I in trouble now?"

"A little."

Judy reached across the table, grasping her lover's hand. "Kathleen darlin', I feel like I'm climbing onto a young colt for the first time. I just don't know what's going to happen, and I'm trying to think through all the possibilities so I'll be ready." Some of the tension went out of Kathleen's face and Judy continued. "You got good taste in people…hell, you're with me, aren't you? I know I'll love this girl, and she's welcome in our home. I'm just hoping it's not a bumpy ride getting where we need to go."

Kathleen laughed. "Since when do you mind a bumpy ride?"

Judy grinned, relieved. "Since the last time I broke a colt. Just wait until Sally Doc Bar's yearling is ready to saddle. You'll see me fidget and sweat then."

Kathleen tilted her head, confused. "You did fine halter breaking. I loved watching that."

"Halter breaking is a contribution to training. Breaking to ride…that's a full commitment. Once on top of a young horse, your life can depend on what happens next."

Kathleen picked up her paper napkin and tore little pieces into a pile by her water glass. "Really?"

"Really."

"You get yourself hurt, Judy Proctor, and I'll have to hurt you some more."

Judy laughed. "I'll do my best to avoid both those disasters."

The waitress/ticket agent looked out the window and spoke to Judy and Kathleen. "Your wait is over. The bus is here."

The two women exited the booth, and Judy stopped to pay their bill while Kathleen walked outside and stood at the curb where she knew the bus would stop. Her face radiated expectation as she awaited her young mentee.

After the bus pulled to a stop, the air brakes gave a loud puff and the door opened for an excited Pookie, who was already standing at the door. The tiny young woman rushed to Kathleen and they hugged and laughed like the soul sisters they were, Kathleen actually picking the girl up off her feet. Judy stepped out of the café and watched, a slow smile easing the tension in her face. The bus driver removed one rolling duffle from the luggage compartment and Judy claimed it for Pookie while the girl and Kathleen hugged and jabbered.

Kathleen set Pookie down and turned to Judy.

"Pookie, you remember Judy, don't you?"

Pookie stood directly in front of Judy, and they looked each other up and down.

"Sure," Pookie said. "I really appreciate you letting me come here."

"You're always welcome. Kathleen claims you as a daughter. That means our home is your home," Judy responded, at the same time noticing the black nail polish and studded dog collar the girl wore.

Punk kid, Judy thought.

Redneck, Pookie thought.

They both gave broad smiles, neither one totally convincing.

Chapter Six

Cow Pies

The sun hovered halfway to the western horizon as they made the forty-minute drive from the Cowboy Café to the ranch. Pookie said little, her backpack holding her most precious items resting on the seat beside her. Even though she was as lithe as a pixie, the step rails on the side of Judy's crew-cab pickup had been a helpful aid when the diminutive Pookie climbed inside. As she drove, Judy glanced in the rear-view mirror and saw the death-grip with which Pookie grasped the handle of the pack. The young woman sat quietly, apparently at ease, but Judy wasn't convinced. The white of Pookie's knuckles reminded her of the feigned nonchalance of rodeo cowboys climbing aboard a one-ton bull.

"Wow!" Pookie said. "It's sure flat around here."

Kathleen laughed. "Big change from the Rocky Mountains, kiddo."

"The cattle like it, and so do I," Judy said, trying hard to keep a defensive edge out of her voice.

Pookie sat silent for several minutes. "It's…it's like the ocean…it's a grand beauty, but…it's a little overwhelming."

Kathleen reached over the console and to the back seat. She squeezed Pookie's knee briefly. "It's going to be okay, Pook."

Judy massaged the steering wheel as she wrestled with conflicting emotions. "This country grows on you," Judy said. "It's back shade country, you know."

"Back shade country?" Pookie asked.

"Yep. If a cowboy decides to rest, he has to sit in the shade of his own back."

Pookie gave a bubbly giggle. For the first time, Judy caught a glimpse of the capacity for happiness in this confusing stranger. Her attention was drawn away from Pookie and back to her driving as a dust devil approached across a pasture and toward the road. A mischievous compulsion made Judy speed-up, ensuring that the truck would be caught in the vortex of the whirlwind. For a moment, even in the heavy truck, there was a confusing sensation of being pulled and pushed in a hundred different directions at once and there was the staccato sound of sand and tumbleweeds hitting the truck.

"Woo-hoo," Pookie yelled. "Can we do that again?"

Judy and Kathleen laughed.

"Sorry, Pookie. Dust devils go where they want and when they want," Judy said. "I can put in an order, but I don't expect the wind gods will pay me no never mind."

Pookie's grip on her backpack eased. "Thanks, Judy. That was awesome."

Kathleen reached across the armrest on the seat that separated her from her lover. Judy took one hand from the wheel and returned the grasp of Kathleen's hand. There was the glisten of tears in Kathleen's eyes when Judy glanced her direction.

"Thank you." Kathleen mouthed the words softly to her lover.

꧁ ꧂

"This is your room," Kathleen said as she pushed open the wooden door to the guest room of the old ranch house.

Pookie paused in the doorway, setting her backpack on the floor and focusing her full attention on the antique glass doorknob. She touched the metal and glass reverently, as though she willed the object to tell its story.

"How old is this place?" Pookie asked.

"Which part?" Kathleen answered. "Judy's great-grandfather first bought land from the Capitol Syndicate in the early 1900s."

"The Capitol Syndicate?"

"This is XIT Ranch Country. When the new State of Texas needed a capital, they sold three million acres at one dollar an acre to a syndicate of buyers—Englishmen, I've heard—who, in exchange, built the capital building in Austin. They worked the XIT Ranch for some time and then sold it off piece by piece to people like Judy's great-grandfather. Ask Judy. She can tell you more."

"You mean I'm living on a real, historic ranch?"

Kathleen laughed. "You sure are." She pushed open the door to Pookie's room and pulled the rolling duffle behind her, speaking over her shoulder as she did. "The original house was just a half-dugout. Your room is part of the first real house her great-grandparents had built…geeze, I think Judy said 1909. Her grandparents and parents each built more onto the main house over the years."

Pookie's mouth hung open. She looked around

the gingerbread woodwork, still its dark-stained original color, where it adorned the liminal space between ceiling and wall. "Wow! Any ghosts?"

"Of course," Kathleen answered, "but the Proctors have always been good souls. I think you'll be safe. You want me to help you unpack?"

"Where did Judy go?" Pookie asked.

"Did you notice the load of cattle feed in the back of the truck?"

"No."

"Judy wanted to unload the feed and take care of the animals in the corrals before dark."

Pookie shifted from foot to foot, uncertain. "Can I help?"

Kathleen motioned for Pookie to grab one end of the duffle. Between them, they lifted the heavy bag onto the bed. Kathleen paused, her head tilted to on side.

"You know, that might be a really good idea. You can unpack later. Why don't you go out to where the truck is parked by the boxcar where we store feed and ask if Judy wants help? I've got an article deadline this week. I wouldn't mind a little time alone to work." Kathleen glanced at her wristwatch. "Besides, it will be getting late by the time all the chores are done. I'll start dinner."

As they walked back through the living room, Pookie paused to look at the painting of a prairie landscape hanging above the couch. It was of an older time, one long gone. A bull buffalo dominated the foreground, his head raised in challenge to the observer, and an inundating sea of his followers covered the gentle slope of rolling prairie behind him. Behind them, a cacophony of orange and yellow and red melded into a sunset with a scattering of clouds in the sky above.

Pookie looked close, realizing it was an original. "Nice work. Who did it?"

"Judy."

Pookie whirled toward Kathleen, her mouth hanging open in shock. "But...but she's a red—" Pookie stopped herself and blushed.

"A redneck?" Kathleen responded. Her face reflected amusement with a hint of aggravation. "Pookie Lugene Thompson, you have a lot to learn."

Pookie blushed. "I...I think I'll go outside now."

In the few minutes she'd been in her new home, Pookie already realized that the front door off the living room was rarely used. She made her way through the kitchen and the mudroom to the back door where she and Kathleen had entered the house. As soon as she was outside, she could see the truck parked across the main yard. It was backed up to the open doors of a retired railroad boxcar, and Judy was working in the truck, throwing fifty pound sacks of cattle feed from the truck one-by-one into the boxcar. Judy paused in her work as she watched Pookie trotting her direction.

"You already settled in?" Judy asked, taking a moment to wipe sweat from her face with the back of her work glove.

"I wanted to help you," Pookie answered.

Judy looked at the young woman, obviously surprised. "This ain't no walk in the park."

"Didn't think it would be," Pookie responded, a glint of defiance in her eyes.

Judy laughed. "Well, climb up here, then. We'll see how you do bringing the bags to the back of the truck, and I'll stack 'em inside. Would save me a lot of time." She looked skeptically at the tiny woman. "These things weigh damn near as much as you."

Pookie had already scrambled into the boxcar and then onto the tailgate. "I'm small but I'm wiry. Played field hockey at school, you know."

Judy grinned devilishly at the girl. "And I'll bet the other teams never forgot you."

"Not if I could help it."

Judy jumped off the tailgate and into the boxcar. "Just bring 'em to me," she said. "No need to carry the full weight. Just drag them to the back of the truck-bed so I can reach them without climbing up and down.

Within moments, the two women had a routine. Judy used her legs as much as possible to lift bags end up, before bending and lifting them to her shoulder so she could carry them to one end of the boxcar where the existing supply of feed cake bags was nearly depleted. With surprising ease, Pookie quickly found her own pull-drag-drop routine; after a few minutes, she had to pause in her work to allow Judy to catch up. After she had pulled the last of the bags to the back of the truck, the wiry little woman hopped into the boxcar and waited for Judy to return for another bag. With no verbal discussion but only the agreement of eye contact, each woman took one end of a feed bag and walked together back to where it was to be stacked.

"Nice job," Judy said as they threw the last bag onto the stack. She caught Pookie's right hand and turned it over to look at it closely. "We need to get you some gloves."

Pookie rubbed at the beginnings of a blister on her forefinger. "That would be nice." She looked at Judy with excitement glinting in her eyes. "What's next, boss?"

Judy shook her head, looking puzzled. "Are you enjoying this?"

"You bet. I'm working on a real, live ranch."

"That you are. That you are. Well, I need to feed the horses and the beef steer we're raising in the pens."

"Can I help?"

Judy looked at the rapidly declining angle of the sun. "Soon you can, but I'd have to teach you who gets what and the pecking order that keeps them from fighting while they eat. Don't really have time before dark."

"I want to do something."

Judy thought for a moment and then reached for an odd, rectangular pitchfork hanging on the wall of the boxcar. She handed it to Pookie.

"What's this?" Pookie asked.

"It's a manure fork."

"A what?"

"A tool for collecting cow pies and horse apples."

Pookie's lip curled in distaste. "Pies and apples? I don't think I want to eat at that kitchen."

Judy gave an honest and long belly laugh. "Pookie, I think you'll do just fine."

"So you want me to clean shit?"

"Yep, and don't you go disparaging prairie coal."

"Prairie what?"

"Come here." Judy motioned for Pookie to follow her out of the boxcar and to look at the prairie before them. "How many trees you see?"

"Ummm…you mean besides the ones in your yard?"

"Yep."

"None."

"When people settled the prairie, what do you

suppose they used to heat their homes and cook their food?"

Pookie looked puzzled. "I never thought about that before. What did they use?"

"Prairie coal…buffalo chips and cow pies mainly."

"You mean they burned manure?"

"They sure did. There was a time when cattle supplied most of the area's heating fuel as well as beef for the nation."

"You're shitting me?"

Judy hesitated before she answered. "Considering the subject, there's no good answer to that, but I'm telling you the truth. It really wasn't until butane and later propane—well, to some extent electricity—came to the area that there really was an alternative for heating and cooking other than manure; burns hot, fast, and clean."

Judy proceed to pontificate some more on the benefits of manure, or, as Kathleen would comment later as she heard the tale, Judy continued to bullshit about bullshit. Maybe it was half a joke as the country woman initiated a city girl, but Pookie listened with rapt attention. The conversation ended abruptly as Judy remembered she still needed to feed before dark. She showed Pookie where the wheelbarrow rested and guided her to a pen empty of animals but well supplied with manure, and she left the girl to work.

Feeding was rushed, but there was still a subdued glow of the end of day when Judy finished. Pookie was just dumping another load of manure as Judy walked to her.

"Good work, young lady. It's time for dinner."

"I want to do a little more."

"You what?"

Pookie looked at Judy, almost pleadingly. "Just a little more, please."

"Well, okay. I'll go in and help Kathleen get the meal. Don't stay long."

Judy pulled off her ball cap and scratched her head, mystified before turning to walk toward the house. As she pulled off her boots in the mudroom, Kathleen approached her lover as she wiped her hands dry on a tea towel. They kissed the brief greeting of comfortable and companionable lovers.

"How'd it go?" Kathleen asked.

"That little girl can work."

"Little ball of fire, isn't she? She'd always get ten times more done than the other kids when we set up for Gay Pride." Kathleen looked at the back door, waiting for it to open. "Where is she?"

"She wanted to do some more work."

"Doing what?"

"Shoveling shit!"

"What? Judy Proctor, if you're trying to initiate that child…"

"Now hold on. I'll admit I was funning a little bit about the importance of cow manure, but before I was done, we both believed it, her a little more than me. She's out there working like she's on a mission."

Kathleen put a fist on each hip and glared at Judy. "Well, get out there and tell her 'mission's accomplished.' Dinner will be ready by the time you've both cleaned up."

Judy took a deep breath, recognizing the tantalizing odor of her wife's chicken enchiladas. "All right, I'll go."

Judy pulled her boots back on and made her way back across the yard to the corrals. There was still enough light that she could see some kind of order to the piles and lines of manure Pookie had arranged.

"What you got going here?" Judy asked as she stepped up to the younger woman.

Pookie pointed first at the largest pile of manure. "That's going to be the buffalo." The pointed along a line of manure to another large pile. "There's the Longhorn," Pookie explained. Another line of manure led to a third, slightly smaller pile. "What's a good modern breed of cattle?"

"My family started out with Herefords. Most folks around here did."

"Herefords then. I've got to figure out how to build the basic structure...maybe wood. Then, I don't know, papier-mache?"

"Adobe is a good filler, and it uses manure in its composition."

"That's a great idea," Pookie said. "What about the structure?"

"You know how to weld?"

"No, but I really want to learn."

"I can teach you." Judy motioned with her chin toward the equipment yard across the county road. "There's nearly a century's worth of scrap metal collected out there. I bet we can find what you need."

They both looked at the piles of manure, suddenly sharing an artistic vision.

"This could work. It could really work," Judy said

"Yeah, it could."

From across the yard, Judy could hear the back door to the house open and the sudden clang of the dinner bell that had hung from the porch roof for as long as she could remember.

"Geeze, I nearly forgot. We better get inside

or Kathleen's going to stew us both for a whole new dinner."

They both walked rapidly across the yard.

"Judy," Pookie said.

"Yeah?"

"I'm really glad Kathleen finally found you."

"Not half as glad as I am that I found her."

Kathleen moved her bookmark to the page she was reading and closed the novel, laying it on the nightstand. She watched her lover enter their bedroom from the adjoining bathroom. Judy wore only an oversized t-shirt as she finished brushing her freshly dried hair. It was her favorite nightshirt, one Kathleen had given her for her birthday. Judy especially loved that it reflected Kathleen's temporary lapse from her usual reserve. Judy was wonderfully surprised as she pulled the shirt from the box to see a large Smiley Face accompanied by the words, 'Boobies make me smile.' Kathleen was not so wonderfully surprised when Judy insisted on actually wearing the shirt almost every night.

"You're not going to let Pookie see that, are you?" Kathleen asked.

"See what?"

"That…shirt."

Judy grinned as she set the hairbrush on her own nightstand. She reached inside the bathroom to turn off the light switch and then crawled between the covers.

"If she's going to live here, she's bound to see it sometime."

Kathleen raised an eyebrow even as she moved to a comfortable position, her head on Judy's shoulder. Both women snaked their arms to familiar positions encircling the other woman. Kathleen let out a mild exclamation of surprise.

"Your feet are cold!"

"Not for long," Judy responded. "I have a top notch foot warmer."

"A foot warmer who is considering a plan to mysteriously move that shirt from the laundry hamper to the trash burn barrel outside."

"Don't you dare! I love this shirt. After all, you gave it to me."

Kathleen sighed and nuzzled at Judy's neck. Her voice was muffled as she spoke against her lover's skin. "Not one of my finer moments."

Judy laughed and lifted Kathleen's chin so that they could kiss, unhurried and with tenderness. "I thought it was a fine gift."

"Sometimes I think embarrassing me by wearing it is part of your pleasure."

"Well…" Judy shrugged.

"Judy Proctor!"

"Darling, you don't give me many good chances to tease you. It's a sign of affection, you know."

"Really?"

"Really."

Kathleen sighed and rested comfortably against Judy. "I'll forgive you under one condition."

"What's that?"

"You wait at least a week before you let Pookie see the shirt and make me confess that I'm the one who bought it."

"Deal." Judy rested her head against the pillows,

thinking. "That Pookie, she's not what I expected."

"I knew you two would like each other, but I didn't expect it to happen this quickly."

"I was damn glad for her help unloading the cattle feed." She flexed the arm that wasn't underneath Kathleen. "I'm a little sore as it is."

Kathleen raised herself on one elbow and gently pushed at her lover. "Roll over. I'll massage your back and shoulders."

Judy did as she was instructed. "A foot warmer and so much more." She moaned softly as Kathleen straddled her lower back and used strong fingers and hands to knead at Judy's sore muscles.

"This would be easier without your shirt."

Judy squirmed slightly as they worked together to pull the controversial nightshirt over her head. Her sigh of satisfaction as Kathleen renewed the kneading was loud enough that Kathleen glanced over her shoulder, toward the closed bedroom door.

"Shhhhh…Pookie will hear," Kathleen said.

Judy's voice was muffled against the pillow. "I think she already has an idea that her mother figure is a lesbian."

"Ha ha. Knowing and actually hearing are two different things."

Judy turned her head to the side so she could be heard. "Damn, I hadn't thought about that part."

"What part?"

"That…that we're the 'moms,' and we're not supposed to let the kid know we actually have sex. I mean, she knows, but she's not supposed to *know*."

Kathleen stopped the massage and moved to lie beside Judy. They faced each other, and Judy reached up to gently stroke Kathleen's hair.

"Did you ever walk in on your parents?" Kathleen asked.

"Once...I was ten. Backed out before they realized I was there. Was three days before I had the guts to talk with my mom about it."

"What did she say?"

"She asked me if I knew how the cows got calves."

"You answered?"

"Of course I knew how."

"Then?"

"Mother asked me if I ever wondered how they got me."

"How did that conversation end?" Kathleen asked.

"Abruptly."

They both laughed, then kissed, long and slow, their hands wandering with gentle familiarity. It might have turned into something more, but it had been a long day. They were tired, and they each drifted to sleep. Over time, the sex had decreased in frequency, but the love making...that was every night and even better over time.

Chapter Seven

Community Meeting

The big folding table in the old one-room schoolhouse was full to overflowing. Juanda Jones' green bean casserole dominated the vegetable portion of the servings, and three of Kathleen's pumpkin empanadas had already mysteriously disappeared even though no one had officially served themselves from the potluck table. A huge brisket, prepared by Julie Kenton (in her mother-in-law's massive slow cooker) was the main entrée. The beef filled the room with a wonderful aroma as it still simmered in the electric cooker, covered in Martha Kenton's secret recipe barbeque sauce. Judy didn't remember a time when either Martha or her own late mother hadn't been the ones to prepare the main meat dish for the monthly Coldwater area community social.

Brad lifted the cover of the cooker for every new arrival, insisting that they smell the contents and informing them that his young wife was standing in as chief cook while his mother was in Amber, awaiting his father's release from the hospital. Judy smiled at his button-busting pride, not bothering to inform anyone of the morning she and Kathleen spent in the Kenton kitchen, providing moral support for Julie as, via the telephone, Martha Kenton walked her young daughter-in-law through every step of the process.

Julie, Judy, and Kathleen all had to swear life-long secrecy before Martha would share her barbeque sauce recipe. Judy laughed so hard she nearly fell on the floor when she learned it was two parts ketchup to one part Worcestershire sauce. She figured her mama was rolling over in her grave. Judy remembered all the years her mother had pestered her best friend for that secret recipe.

When Pookie learned of the potluck, she insisted on making her signature cauliflower hummus with green olives. Judy gently reminded Pookie that ranch folk tended to be meat and potatoes kind of people, but Judy's doubts ended as soon as she tasted the concoction. Good was good, even if it was some new-fangled hummus with bagel chips.

"What's this?" Curley Thomas asked as Pookie set the dish on the table, opening the bag of bagel chips and scattering them on the plate around the bowl of hummus.

"It's hummus," Pookie answered.

Curley looked at the bowl from the left, the right, up, and down.

"Ain't that hippie food?" he asked.

"Some folks think so," Judy answered as she moved closer, ready to intercede if Pookie felt threatened.

"Got any of that Mary Jane in it?"

Pookie laughed. "No. No marijuana in it."

"Damn," Curley said. "Always wanted to try me some of that stuff."

Pookie drew some interesting stares when they first arrived at the former schoolhouse. There was a noted moment of silence as the young woman walked into the room, dressed in her finest dog collar, all black clothes, and a crystal stud glinting from her eyebrow piercing. Purple, spikey hair topped off the outfit, and she was back in her ragged, black fashion jeans, her new Levis left at home.

Judy stepped into the middle of the room, her hand on Pookie's shoulder. Judy stood tall and spoke loud.

"Hi, y'all," she said. "This is Pookie Thompson, and she'll be living with Kathleen and me for a while. Treat her right. She's good folks and like a daughter to Kathleen."

Kathleen, holding her platter of empanadas, moved to Judy's right and Brad stepped immediately to her left. The three formed a protective semi-circle around Pookie.

The following silence was brief.

"Well, don't just stand there, child," said old Mrs. Haskell. "Come in and make yourself at home."

The old woman was almost as small as Pookie and somewhat shorter than she'd been in her younger years, before the osteoporosis bowed her spine. She walked to Pookie, and put her hand gently on the young woman's arm, leading Pookie toward the food table. The cacophony of laughter and conversation resumed, although curious glances continued toward the newcomer.

Being summer time, dinner had to wait while the younger folks undertook a game of softball outside, a game with more enthusiasm than skill and more laughter than rules. Curley was already on his third beer before he assumed the role of scorekeeper. When the game was called for dinner after a couple of innings, he was pretty sure the score was five to three, but he couldn't remember which team had which score.

Pookie's differences were largely forgotten after she hit a triple, causing Brad to dive for the ball and ending up in a patch of sand burrs. His team was short-handed for a while as he and Julie exited to the schoolhouse's tiny bathroom so she could extract the ones lodged in his left butt-cheek. Nobody won. Nobody lost. Nobody cared. It was about time together, solitary ranchers and farmers remembering that their homes may be scattered and distant, but they were still a community.

After the game, the gathering of nearly thirty country folk descended on the food table like a horde of locusts. Every woman and few of the men always brought their specialty dishes, and people generally knew their favorites from many times before. Rarely was there much left, and this evening would be no exception. Plates were filled and many still abided by Mrs. Haskell's long-standing insistence that if you never emptied your plate, it wasn't seconds. Judy was relieved to see that Pookie's hummus was going along with all the other old favorites. At first, a few polite spoonfuls disappeared, but greater quantities went as folks came back for non-seconds. The hummus had passed the test, and Judy was beginning to hope that so had Pookie. Her good-naturedness at softball helped, but it was something more. Kathleen was still confused as to how local people could be so conservative and yet accept Judy and Kathleen, knowing they partook in the sin that dare not be named. Judy tried to explain, but somehow, it always fell short.

❧ ❧ ❧

"It's…it's like testing a horse," Judy said one night late as they lie in bed, discussing the paradox for the thousandth time.

Kathleen rose onto one elbow and looked at her lover, an eyebrow raised. "Not sure I like being compared to a mare."

"More like a filly," Judy responded.

"Aren't I a little old for that?"

"Oh hell, you're missing the point. Just listen for a minute."

"Okay, okay."

"My daddy loved Quarterhorses...all we ever had, all we ever rode, but no matter what the breed, what's most important is the individual horse. Yes, confirmation and muscle tone, strength, and intelligence all enter into it, but in the end, the thing that matters most is what they have in their heart. The only way to know that is to handle 'em, ride 'em, see what they're made of. Only then do you know if you can trust 'em, rely on 'em. If you can, well, who cares if it's an Arab, or a Morgan instead of a Quarterhorse?"

"I'm still not tracking, honey," Kathleen said.

"Sweetheart, these folks know they can count on us. We're real to them. They know what we're made of, and we've been found to be sound, worthy to run with the herd."

"But they think it's a sin...that we're sinners... even Martha and Harold...even Brad."

"Yes, they do. It's a paradox."

"How do they resolve that within themselves?"

Judy laughed, pulling Kathleen to her, nuzzling into her hair. "I guess it's because we're their sinners and they love us."

Kathleen laughed and moaned slightly as Judy nibbled at that special spot at the base of her skull. "You're changing the subject."

"Yes, I am," Judy responded. She continued the conversation with her hands and mouth, and Kathleen soon willingly accepted the new communication.

❧ ❧ ❧ ❧

Judy glanced toward Pookie, watching the young woman work with Kathleen gathering dirty dishes from around the room. When all the plates were scraped clean into the oversized trashcan, Pookie volunteered to carry the trash bag out to the bed of Judy's truck so that she could throw it at the nearby county dump-station on their way home. Judy worked with Brad, sponging off and gathering vinyl table clothes and reconfiguring the room from meal time to game time. Pookie was proving she had what it took, and the local folks were already welcoming her to the herd. In a few short weeks, Judy had gone from skeptical to grateful that Kathleen allowed her to share a parenting role for this unusual young woman. Judy had assumed that, in time, both the Proctor and the Kenton Ranches would pass to Brad and Julie's children. As she watched Pookie weave her way into the Coldwater community, while still maintaining her own somewhat rebellious persona, Judy wasn't so sure that the future of her home rested entirely in Kenton hands. Time would tell.

The community worked like a well-oiled machine. It didn't take long for the dishes to be washed, dried, and put away, and the tables were set up for a smorgasbord of games from which to choose. Dominoes for regular dominoes and 42, a full over-sized set for those who wanted chicken foot, and decks of cards were on other tables for bridge, hearts, or gin rummy. Judy and Kathleen settled down to a game of chicken foot with Brad and Julie, and Pookie wandered the room, watching the different games, but not choosing to play.

"Hey Judy, may I have the keys to the truck?" Pookie asked.

"Sure, but why?" Judy started digging in her pocket.

"I left my sketchpad, pencils, and pastels out there."

"It's not locked. Just go get your stuff."

Pookie laughed. "I still forget we're not in the city."

"Aren't you having fun, Pook?" Kathleen asked.

"Having a great time, but I want to finish something I was working on today."

Nobody paid much attention when Pookie came back inside and sat at an unoccupied card table, her back to the wall. She spread out her sketchpad and other art supplies and set to work. Although various people cast curious glances, it was hard to get a feel for the art while looking at it from a flattened angle and upside-down. Brad being Brad, as soon as they finished the game of chicken foot, he left the table and looked over Pookie's shoulder.

"Well, I'll be!" he called. "Judy Proctor, you got some serious competition here as our resident artist."

"Tell me about it," Judy replied. "Girl's got talent."

"Come lookie here," Brad said.

Half the occupants of the room accepted Brad's invitation, and numerous games were abandoned. Judy noticed Pookie's blush as the group gathered. Judy looked at the picture and recognized it immediately as a visual rendition of Pookie's vision for the sculpture she began planning the first night she arrived at the ranch. Judy was impressed. Pookie had obviously done her research. The buffalo, Longhorn, and Hereford were correct in every detail, although the Hereford was still a sketch with a few flashes of color, unfinished. Tying all three together was a line of shit, starting as flaming and progressing to golden shit, magical shit... Pookie had obviously taken to heart Judy's lecture about the importance of prairie coal.

Brad picked up the art on Pookie's oversized sketchpad and held it up for all to see.

"That's mighty fine work, girl," Curley said, and the group murmured agreement.

"It's going to be a sculpture," Pookie said.

"That's pretty awesome," Brad said.

"Where you going to put it?" Mrs. Haskell asked.

"She's got a place picked out by the corrals at our place," Judy answered.

Pookie stood up, turning her art back toward herself so she could study it more closely. "Judy's going to teach me to weld to build the frame for each of the animals. We talked about maybe using adobe with a glazed finish for the exterior."

"Be kind of a waste just at your corrals," Brad said.

"Sure would." Curley's face shone with a bright smile. "Why don't you build it right here in front of the community center?"

"What a great idea," one rancher said.

"I agree," his wife added.

"All those in favor say 'aye,'" Curley called.

The vote was unanimous. So began the Coldwater area's first community art project.

Chapter Eight

Homecoming

It was a good thing the Kentons had a farm yard. No regular suburban home could handle the parking. Not just the Coldwater folks turned out for Harold's homecoming. Half the church choir from the Dulson First Baptist Church was there, along with their minister. They'd certainly missed Harold's bass voice these many Sunday mornings. Three members of the Dulson County Farmers' Cooperative board of directors were there, including Chub Smithson, who drove all the way from his farm near Conway, clear on the other side of the county. To no one's surprise, Fire Chief Rome was there along with Sally Lyne, the volunteer EMT who had treated Harold when he was burned. During his time in the hospital, Sally called almost every week just to see how he was doing.

Brad and Julie were busy making coffee and tea for all the visitors, and the house was full to overflowing. In the kitchen, the table and counters rapidly filled with pies, casseroles, and homemade bread. Country folk know how to express love and caring in a very practical way. The recuperating Harold and his worry weary wife wouldn't need to be concerned about feeding themselves for a while. Judy and Kathleen stayed outside, greeting newcomers and directing parking, reminding folks not to park by the front gate to the house. They wanted the path kept clear to make Harold's last few steps on the final leg of his journey home as easy as possible.

During their last trip to Amber, Judy and Kathleen found Harold to be restless and grumpy. Martha's patience was obviously wearing thin. After the third time Martha referred to her beloved husband as a "cantankerous old coot," Judy offered to stay with Harold while Martha and Kathleen, with Pookie in tow, went to lunch and then to the mall. Martha got an over-due haircut and came back with a brand new shirt for Harold, one from the western wear store and just the color and style he liked. When he saw it, tears came to his eyes, the first Judy had seen from the tough and weathered rancher since her own parents' funeral.

While they were alone, Judy listened as Harold ranted, worried about the ranch, worried about hospital bills, feeling as trapped as a steer left forgotten in a branding squeeze chute. He calmed after a while. His burns had largely healed, although the doctor warned him he needed to be watchful of the delicate new skin around both the graft and on his thigh where they'd taken healthy skin to replace burned tissue. The knee replacement had gone well, and Harold amazed them all in the hospital physical therapy department with how well he progressed. He wanted to go home, pure and simple. Harold knew he was ready, and he was frustrated at the doctors' caution in keeping him longer.

After he'd settled some, Judy described how well the wheat looked on both their places, wheat planted for the winter grazing, but always welcome as a secondary cash crop when the rains were enough to make it worth harvesting. She and Brad had already contracted a harvest crew from Abilene. They would be in the Dulson area in a week or two as they followed the ripening wheat from south to north. By the time she started her update on the successful calving of the heifers—having lost only one premature calf—Harold was more his old self, the calm and steady man who was a second father to her.

The day had finally arrived. Harold would be home in less than an hour. He'd called from their cell phone, Martha driving, telling Brad to have the coffee on and his worn-out recliner ready to welcome the 'master' home. Brad did a little jig at the sound of his father's excited voice, then took a marker and paper from the table near the phone in the kitchen. He wrote "RESERVED" in bold letters and unceremoniously ran Curley Thompson out of his father's favorite chair, placing the sign in the middle of the seat.

When the Kentons' Buick pulled into the yard, a cheer went up, starting with a small group of men resting and whittling under a shade tree. The people in the house heard the commotion, and Brad and Julie abandoned their guests to run to meet his parents. People lined up along the sidewalk, shouting things like "welcome home" and "you look darned good, Harold."

Harold and Martha were both grinning ear-to-ear as they stepped from the car. Harold carried a cane, but he forgot to use it as he walked, limping ever so slightly. He shook hands, calling the names of his many friends as he made that longed-for walk into his own house on his own ranch. Martha barely got out of the car before some of her lady friends from church waylaid her with tearful hugs. Judy gently slipped the car keys from Martha's hand. She hit the button on the key fob to open the trunk, and she and

Kathleen quietly retrieved suitcases and bags from the trunk. They waited for the crowd to clear, one-by-one following Harold and Martha into the house. Instead of following the group through the front door, Judy and Kathleen took the bags to the back porch, went through the kitchen, down the hallway, and deposited bags in the Kentons' bedroom. It sounded like a New Year's celebration from the laughter and loud conversation in the living room. It truly was a day of celebration.

There had to be twenty people gathered around Harold, now seated in his favorite chair, Martha in her own chair beside him. Judy and Kathleen didn't even try to make their way through the crowd. Despite their presence on the outskirts, Martha searched for them, making eye contact and mouthing the words "thank you." Judy winked in response and Kathleen waved.

"Darned if I don't smell home cooking coming from that kitchen," Harold said, his face beaming with happiness.

"Brought two loaves of my homemade yeast bread," Mrs. Haskell called.

"You got enough food to feed an army in there," Curley said.

"Good thing," Martha responded, "'cause we pretty near have an army in our living room."

"You listen here, Martha Kenton. That food is for you. You don't need to feed all us," said a dumpling looking woman Judy didn't know. *Must be from the church*, Judy thought.

"Well, I'm not offering," Harold said. "After all those weeks on hospital food, I may eat myself into oblivion on all that good food."

Sally Lyne, wearing her EMT vest, stepped to a spot beside Harold. "Harold, we're all glad to see you, but don't you overdo it, including the eating."

Harold stood, a full head taller than the woman beside him. He put a hand on Sally's shoulder and looked into her eyes.

"There's my angel," he said, his voice shaky. "The angel who was there for me at my darkest hour."

He wrapped Sally in a gentle hug, one he seemed disinclined to end. Martha stood and wrapped her arms around them both. Sally finally stepped away, swiping quickly at her eyes with the sleeve of her shirt.

"What you talking about? I was just doing my job," she said.

"I'll never forget what you did for me." Harold looked up, searching the faces in the room until he spotted Fire Chief Rome. "Ted, I won't forget what all you folks in the fire department did that day," he said, speaking directly to the Chief.

"Harold, your son and Judy Proctor over there --" The Chief used his chin to point to Judy at the back of the group, "have been busy while you were in the hospital." He held up an over-sized brown envelope. "What I have here is authorization from the Dulson County Commissioners and the State Fire Marshall's office for the charter of the Coldwater Volunteer Fire Department."

"We did it for you, Dad," Brad said. "We don't want a day like the day you got burned ever again, for anyone."

Big, tough, weather-beaten cowhand that he was, Harold Kenton cried. His wife cried. The dumpling lady from their church cried. Judy cried. Kathleen cried. Pretty much everyone cried, although most of the tougher men managed to hide it in the form of a bout of unexpected coughing.

"That's not all, Harold," said Joe Bob Johnston, foreman of the Bar H, the biggest ranch in the area. He pulled at his bushy mustache in a nervous gesture. "You know my boss, Bob Hanks."

"Sure I do. Who doesn't? Most of Texas knows he's an oil man's oil man. Seemed like a nice enough fellow when you two came in for coffee when you were pheasant hunting."

Joe Bob looked around the room. Most times, the big cowboy didn't speak much. Judy had never seen him nervous before. She doubted he was particularly comfortable making a public announcement.

"Mr. Hanks, well, he heard about the fire, and he got downright motivated when he learned how far it was to the nearest fire station. Anyway, he's agreed to donate the money to build us a firehouse. Been talking with folks, and we figure it can go beside the Community Center."

"And we've already located a used Class A pumper and a former State Forestry brush truck you can use until we can get grants for new equipment," Chief Rome added.

"Yippee!" Brad called. He grabbed Julie and tried to lead her in a dosey-doe, but there wasn't enough room in the crowded living room.

Judy grasped Kathleen's hand, as happy as Brad over it all, but a bit more self-restrained. Kathleen leaned close to her lover.

"Looks like you and Brad really started something," Kathleen whispered.

"We sure did," Judy responded. Somewhere mixed in her joy for the day, there was a cold kernel of fear. *A firefighter*, Judy thought. *Damn, a firefighter.*

"That's enough excitement for today," Sally Lyne

said, authority in the voice of the diminutive woman. "All you folks need to go home and let this man rest."

Obediently, everyone did as they were told.

❧ ❧ ❧ ❧

As they pulled into the drive at their own headquarters, Kathleen changed direction from house to corrals after she spotted Pookie riding Old Buck in the arena behind the pens.

"That darned hat," Judy said as she watched the young rider.

"Well, you told her she had to wear a hat if she was going to be out working. You even gave her the money to buy it," Kathleen said.

"Where in the hell did she actually find a derby? I hadn't seen one of those in years."

Kathleen parked the car where they could watch Pookie ride. "Did you really expect Pookie to buy a nice, practical hat?"

"I was all ready for a ball cap that said 'Save the Whales' or some such, but a derby…never imagined."

"It goes well with her hair."

"That it does, and the black hat goes good with the black of her dog collar." Judy watched in silence for a few minutes as Pookie loped the horse in a big figure eight. "She's doing good on Old Buck."

"Same horse I learned to ride on, but you know Pookie rode before."

"She told me she had a pony, but sometimes learning to ride badly is worse than not learning to ride at all," Judy said. "She's got a good touch and a solid seat." She reached to take Kathleen's hand. "Still not as much of a natural as you were from the get go."

"You going to leave her on Old Buck?" Kathleen asked.

Judy rubbed at her chin, thinking. "I been thinking about getting another horse for you. You're ready for one with a little more spunk. We could put Pookie on Dan."

Kathleen laughed. "Just so you don't expect me to rope any cattle. I'm afraid a good horse could lose me by accident."

"Well, Jackson's done that to me a time or two."

"I know. I helped clean up and bandage your scraped face the last time, remember?" Kathleen laughed. "Why do you think I'm so certain a good horse would lose me?"

Judy opened the door to the car. "We'll see," she said as she and Kathleen both stepped out of the vehicle. She looked at Kathleen over the top of the car. "I'll ask Joe Bob to keep an eye out for another good but gentle horse. Truthfully, I'm thinking about asking him to start Sally's colt for me. I don't bounce as good as I used to, and that round-pen of his is perfect for starting to saddle train a young horse."

Kathleen sighed and leaned wistfully on the car. "Oh please, Judy. I'd feel so much better if you did."

Judy smiled, glancing sideways at her lover. "We'll see."

Pookie rode up to the fence and pulled Old Buck to a stop. "How'd it go?" she asked.

"Great!" Kathleen answered. "You missed a good time."

"I would have felt funny. I saw how Mr. Kenton looked at me when I went with you to the hospital. I did have fun hanging out with Mrs. Kenton though."

Judy laughed. "Give him time. Although you

better be darned glad Martha didn't take your advice about dying her hair. Harold would have roasted you both alive."

"She'd look good blond…maybe with a streak of blue."

Judy sighed and shook her head. "It's your turn to cook tonight, kiddo. What we having?"

"I have lentils in the crock pot with some Cajun spice, and maybe a nice salad with poppy-seed dressing."

"Sounds…good," Judy responded.

Judy and Kathleen got back in the car and Kathleen drove them to the driveway by the house.

"Kathleen?" Judy said as they drove.

"Yes?"

"What are lentils?" Judy asked. "Some kind of meat?"

Kathleen laughed so hard she couldn't answer.

Chapter Nine

Young Love

It was a long drive to Amber. Pookie rode quietly in the backseat of Kathleen's car, so quietly that the two women in front kept sneaking glances at her in the mirror or over their shoulders.

"What's up, Pook?" Kathleen finally asked.

"Well…we're going to Amber," Pookie answered.

"I know that," Kathleen drawled. She turned around in the driver's seat and looked at Pookie over the top of her sunglasses.

"Sometimes it pays to state the obvious," Pookie said. She didn't look at Kathleen, instead staring at the arroyos around the Canadian River as they hurled along the state highway between Dulson and the city of Amber.

"All right, kiddo. Why so quiet?" Judy asked, a hint of authority in her voice.

Pookie chewed briefly on her lower lip. "You say they call it the Ladies' Room?"

"Yep," Judy answered.

"And they're all lesbians?"

"Lesbian or gay friendly," Judy answered.

Kathleen giggled. "Wait until you meet Sara Jean."

"Who's that?" Pookie asked.

Judy laughed so hard she snorted. "She's some

bow-head, rich house wife who came the first time because she thought the 'lambda ladies' were a meeting of her college sorority alumni."

"She comes back to get advice from the lesbians on how to deal with her husband and her flirty neighbor," Kathleen added.

Pookie laughed too, taking her gaze from the passing scenery and looking toward her companions. "Sounds like fun, but...well..."

"Spit it out," Judy said.

"Are there any...you know...girls?"

Judy and Kathleen exchanged a quick "ah-ha" glance. "Pookie Thompson, are you hoping to find a girlfriend?" Kathleen asked.

"Well, yeah." Pookie unfastened her seatbelt and leaned forward into the space between the two front bucket seats, placing her hands on the shoulders of the two women. "You know...well...it's been a while."

Judy's mouth hung open, and she turned to face Pookie. "How old are you?" she demanded.

"You know how old I am. I turned eighteen in March," Pookie responded.

Judy huffed in disdain. "I'll have you know I didn't get around to doing 'it' until I was in my twenties. And fasten your seat belt," Judy said.

Doing as instructed, Pookie scooched back in her seat and re-buckled the belt. "Times have changed, Miz Judy. Times have changed."

"Well, I think waiting until you're a little older is a good thing," Judy said. "Don't you agree, Kathleen?"

All three listened attentively to the hum of tires on the pavement.

"Kathleen?" Judy said.

More tires on pavement.

"Kathleen, honey. How old were you the first time you…well…did 'it'?"

Kathleen cleared her throat. "Pookie, there's a wide range of ages among the women at the Ladies' Room. We kind of bonded with some of the adult couples, so, I'm sorry, sweetie, I didn't notice how many unattached young women were there."

Judy put a hand on the dashboard and leaned her back against the door, facing Kathleen directly. "You're not going to answer my question, are you?"

"Not in front of Pookie, no."

Judy licked her lips and nodded. "Fair enough, but we will talk later."

"Hey!" Pookie called. "No mom fights are allowed on account of me."

The two women laughed. "Not a fight, sweetie. Just a slightly uncomfortable…discussion," Kathleen responded.

Judy sighed. "I guess I'm not a good standard to go by. After all, I spent my life until college just on the ranch, riding a bus to school until I was sixteen. Even after Brad and I started driving his dad's old pickup into town for high school so he could do football, and I could do band…well, I guess if I'd had opportunity, it might have been different."

Kathleen breathed a loud sigh of relief. "Opportunity certainly does make a difference."

Pookie leaned as far forward as she possibly could without releasing her seatbelt. "So, did either of you ever do it with a guy?"

"Pookie, sweetie," Kathleen said.

"Yes?"

"Shut up."

They listened to tire hum for a time, until Judy

started to giggle. Pookie out-and-out laughed.

"This is *not* the kind of game of twenty questions I want to answer on a road trip," Kathleen said, smiling despite the disdain in her voice. "I'll bet we're close enough to Amber to get the Country station," she said.

Kathleen punched the radio "on" button then the pre-set button for the desired station, turning up the volume when music was heard. Judy raised the plastic cover on the passenger sun-visor, exposing the mirror. She looked directly at Pookie in the seat behind her and gave the younger woman a brazen wink. Pookie held her breath, holding in her laughter.

❧❧❧❧

Pookie walked up the wooden stairs behind her moms. She carried a platter of the stuffed jalapenos she and Kathleen had made while Judy was outside moving the horses out of the corrals into the horse pasture and shutting Somegood and Useless into the barn where they were well supplied with extra food and water. They'd be spending the night in Amber, guests of Judy and Kathleen's friends, April and Sophia. Brad would check dogs, horses, and cattle in the morning, and the three women were free for a real girls' night out.

Pookie had been equal parts eager and anxious from the moment Judy first suggested they all go to Amber for the weekly Ladies' Room meeting. She'd been comfortable with the group of young people in the gay-straight alliance from her high school, the group that enabled her to find Kathleen as her mentor and lesbian mom. She'd known some of them since kindergarten, and it had been an easy transition from school to being the gay clique. Pookie usually found it easy to meet new people. Even as a young child, her father had always brought her along, meeting clients, friends, and other artists, even his buddies at the golf course. Still, this was something new. She and her friends had wheedled their way into a gay bar in Colorado Springs a time or two, and Pookie figured she'd even be more comfortable in the noise and anonymity of the Pink Triangle. In the Ladies' Room, women would talk, tell their stories, maybe even expose their souls. As she stood outside the open door, she could hear Judy and Kathleen inside, greeting their new friends; Pookie felt…well…naked.

A shorthaired woman wearing a Texas Tech t-shirt and faded jeans stepped out the door and smiled warmly.

"Get on in here, Pookie." The woman extended her hands, taking the platter of jalapenos with one and grasping Pookie's right hand in a firm handshake with the other. "I'm April Sims. Judy and Kathleen have told us a lot about you."

"Good, I hope."

April laughed. "I'd tell you, but it might give you a big head."

Pookie returned the handshake warmly, feeling still naked but a lot safer in being so. She stepped inside.

The room was warm, in more ways than one. A window unit air conditioner cranked away in the tiny kitchen area, but it was taxed to keep up with the combined heat of a roomful of animated women, laughing and talking in a cacophony of sound. Pookie scanned the room, and she liked what she saw. It felt safe here, warm, like…like a hearth where she could take refuge. There were grey-haired women, young women, bold butches, and flashy fems, a whole variety of women, and they all belonged. It showed in the ease with which they talked and the relative lack of personal space with women leaning close to each other, striving to hear their individual conversations over the din of sound. There was even one man, looking more like a church deacon than a gay guy, and Pookie felt certain the woman beside him, a hand softly on his forearm, had to be his wife. The women around them seemed perfectly at ease with the couple, and the complexity of the situation momentarily confused Pookie.

Pookie didn't complete her scan of the room. It ended abruptly when her gaze fell on one woman, a girl really, with auburn hair and green eyes and a gentle way of moving her hands as she spoke to an older woman dressed in a softball jersey. The girl looked up and their gazes locked like machine parts finding home when the right piece fit with the right piece. Pookie was oblivious to the wordless message between Judy and Kathleen, shared eye contact alone expressing their joint awareness of Pookie's focus on the auburn-haired girl.

"Come on, Pook," Judy said, placing a hand on Pookie's elbow and gently guiding her. "April starts the discussion right at seven. Let's find our seats."

Judy and Kathleen performed a subtle dance, positioning themselves to seats on a couch, one where there was only room for them. Pookie barely noticed. The auburn-haired girl had finally dropped her gaze, but Pookie still stared, totally fascinated.

"The younger ones usually sit on the floor," Kathleen explained to Pookie, gently pushing on Pookie's shoulders and guiding her to a seat in front of them. The older, straight couple moved to two chairs beside the couch, and Pookie thought her heart might burst right out of her chest as the auburn-haired girl moved to take a seat on the floor in front of them, a place just inches from where Pookie now sat.

Judy leaned forward, speaking to the two young girls. "Pookie, I want you to meet Terry. Terry, this is our dear, young friend, Pookie."

The girl looked shyly toward her own shoes, pulling her knees up under her chin and wrapping her arms around her legs. She blushed. In that instant, Pookie wanted nothing more than to put this shy young woman at ease. She extended her hand and smiled her most charming smile.

"Hello, Terry. I'm really, really glad to meet you."

The girl blushed more, but she raised her eyes to gaze directly at Pookie. Pookie was afraid she might drown in the deep, sea green color of those eyes.

"Happy to meet you," the girl said.

From across the room, April started clanking a butter knife against a glass. The noise dwindled.

"All right ladies, oh, and you, Mr. Jones. You all know the drill. It's time for our group discussion," April said.

"She would have made a fine drill sergeant, don't you think?" an older woman said, ending her statement with a playful wink.

A beautiful Latina sitting in the chair beside April took April's hand and leaned toward April. "I love it when she tries to command me," the woman said.

April raised her eyebrows in a Groucho Marx expression. "And I love the way she says 'no,'" she announced to the room at large.

Kathleen leaned toward Pookie, whispering in her ear. "That's April and Sophia, the ones we'll stay with tonight."

Pookie managed to pull her awareness away from the girl long enough to actually look at and see her hostesses. She nodded understanding toward Kathleen.

"Tonight's going to be a little different, if no one objects," April said. "We have special guests. I think most of you remember Alfred and Martha Jones, co-presidents of the local PFLAG organization." The older couple sitting near them waved shyly at the group, and the women smiled or waved in return. The man cleared his throat and took a deep breath before speaking.

"You may know that we've been meeting with the Amber Superintendent of Schools off and on for over a year now. He's still not ready to make the Gay-Straight Alliance an official organization at the school, but he has agreed to let us coordinate some awareness training for teachers."

Martha Jones leaned forward and gently stroked the auburn hair of the young girl sitting in front of her. "If we can help it, we don't want anyone else to go through what Terry or her Marilyn went through."

Tears appeared in Terry's eyes. Without any conscious decision to do so, Pookie reached over and took the girl's hand, giving it a comforting squeeze. The green gaze turned directly toward Pookie. Pookie couldn't breathe. In that moment, she believed she would never see anything more beautiful nor more heartbreaking than those tear-filled eyes. To Pookie's amazement, Terry returned the squeeze and continued to hold onto Pookie's hand. Pookie left her hand resting warmly in the tentative embrace.

Alfred Jones picked up the narrative. "Anyway, Martha and I can help coordinate sensitivity training for the teachers, but it's not our stories to tell. We need help from some of you."

A stout woman in a Cowboys football t-shirt spoke. "Heck, I retired last year after coaching softball and basketball and teaching science at West Side High School for thirty years. I'll talk to them."

"That's awesome, Mo," April said. "Alfred, Martha, you know Sophia and I will help all we can."

"April, we were rather hoping you'd kind of organize and spearhead who will do the talking and what they need to say," Alfred confessed.

"Drill sergeant...I told you. She'd make an awesome drill sergeant," the older woman said.

April gave the woman a sly smile. "Quit picking on me, Tandy. You're the one who drafted me to organize the Ladies' Room in the first place."

"And a fine job you've done, old friend. A fine job."

"I'll do it," a soft voice said. The room went quiet and everyone looked at Terry.

Martha stroked the girl's hair once again. "I know it's painful, honey. You don't have to."

Terry sat up straight, her soft voice still quiet but strong. "I'm the one who was kicked out on the streets when I was sixteen. I'm the one who...whose lover hung herself because of the persecution. These teachers need to know. They need to see the price of prejudice in school and church and home."

"Damn," Pookie whispered to herself. She wished with all her heart she were a time traveling Wonder Woman, someone who could zip back to the past and protect this girl, this person who was already precious to her.

Talk continued, but Pookie didn't hear much. Somehow, she and Terry shifted positions on the floor.

They didn't touch nor embrace, but Terry was close enough for Pookie to feel the warmth of her, even to catch a whiff of her perfume. It was an agonizing heaven, one that befuddled her brain and made her unable to follow the group conversation. She barely had enough presence of mind to collect herself and say, "thanks for the welcome" when she realized she was being introduced. When the discussion ended, and everyone headed for the potluck dinner, Pookie stood, still close and facing Terry.

"I'm…I'm so sorry about…about what happened to you and to…"

"To Marilyn," Terry said.

"Was that your lover?"

"Yes. We both went to the same church…Alfred and Martha were there too. There was this nasty, nasty preacher. He hated gays."

"Such a fine Christian attitude."

"Especially since it turned out he was a pedophile too." Terry looked across the room toward where April and Sophia were filling their plates. "Thanks to April, he got caught. He's in jail now."

Pookie looked toward April, seeing the woman in a new way. "Bet he was sorry he messed with the drill sergeant."

Terry laughed. "How did you do that?"

"Do what?"

"Make me laugh."

"Just a knack I guess. Life's funny, even when it's not. Know what I mean?"

Terry looked at Pookie quizzically. "Not yet, but I'd sure like a chance to figure it out."

Pookie interpreted Terry as saying she wanted to get to know Pookie better. The joy shone on Pookie's face as she responded. "I'll be happy to teach you what little I know about life and laughter and stuff."

"You're the one from Colorado who came to live with Judy and Kathleen, right?"

"Yep. I got kicked out too, but no streets for me. Straight from city to ranch, and I love it."

Terry looked at Pookie's now blue hair, a break from the former purple, and piercings then toward Judy's cowboy boots and blue jeans.

"You and Judy get along?" Terry asked.

"She's the best, along with Kathleen."

"I always thought Judy looked a little like… well…"

"A redneck?"

"Yes."

"Looks can be deceiving." Pookie raised her five foot, one inch frame to its full height. "Bet you'd never guess I'm a genuine cowhand now."

Terry tilted her head, studying Pookie. "No, not at all. I can tell it's going to be a lot of fun getting to know you."

"The feeling is very, very mutual."

❧❧❧❧

Inside, the cacophony of conversation and laughter had returned to the pre-formal meeting decibel level. The crowd descended like a starving horde on the table holding the usual fine food of a lesbian potluck. With full plates, they settled throughout the room to eat, talk, and laugh. After filling their own plates, Pookie and Terry found their way outside to the relative privacy of the wooden, exterior stairs. They shared a step for their seat and used a higher step as their table. For Pookie, it felt like an oasis, a small bubble of semi-quiet between the noise of the Ladies' Room and the deep rumble of DJ music from the bar below. It felt intimate.

"How long will you be staying with Kathleen and Judy?" Terry asked.

"No plans beyond tomorrow," Pookie answered. "But it will be a few months at least. Judy and I are doing a sculpture for the Coldwater community center."

"You're kidding."

"No joke, but some people might think it is. You see, it's…well, it's kind of in honor of prairie coal."

"Prairie coal?" Terry asked, her faced tilted to one side in the universal gesture of curiosity.

"Buffalo and cow shit."

"What?"

"Yeah. The first evening I arrived, Judy was telling me about manure being the only fuel early settlers had for their fires. The Colt Peacemaker may have settled the West, but it was shit that warmed it, at least on the prairie."

Terry dropped her fork in her plate and sat with her mouth open in surprise. "Geeze, I work at the High Plains Museum at the university and I never, ever wondered about what people used for fire fuel on the treeless plains."

"Was kind of a surprised to me too, but it gave me an idea." Pookie sighed in mild frustration. "If I'd known I'd meet you and we'd be talking about my project, I would have brought my art pad with the conceptual drawings."

"Describe it."

"It starts with a buffalo, then a Longhorn, and ends in a Hereford, each of them tied together by a trail of fire…not real fire, you know…a sculpture of fire."

"Sounds ambitious, and the fire should be a lot more…attractive…than a trail of poop."

"We'll build the basic shapes of the animals from scrap metal and chicken wire. Judy's teaching me to weld, then we'll finish out with adobe, plaster, and paint. Still working on exactly how I'll do the trail of fire."

"Wow, Pookie. You're a real artist."

The bite of potato salad on Pookie's fork paused halfway to her mouth. Her eyes focused into a distance of time rather than space.

"My dad was the artist."

"Was?"

"Yeah…he died in a car wreck when I was eleven."

"I'm so sorry."

"I miss him, but it would have been an even greater tragedy if he'd never been my dad at all."

"I envy you."

Pookie was surprised. "What?"

"Sounds like your dad would have done anything for you."

"He would have and me for him." Pookie remembered the bit of food she still held mid-air and placed it in her mouth.

Terry pushed the food around on her plate. "My parents threw me out of the house when they found out I was a lesbian." Terry looked up the stairs toward the closed door of the Ladies' Room. "The women here, they saved me. I lived with Mo and went to her high school until I graduated. She even got me the job at the museum and helped me get a grant so I could go to college. Others helped me out too, and April…geeze…

April's the one who stopped the bastard minister who told my parents they had to kick me out or go to hell."

"Oh, Terry. I'm so sorry you had to go through that."

"I'm not. Being gay saved me. It saved me from being some passive little Christian lady, constantly afraid of living, afraid of hell and damnation."

"You go girl."

"Pookie."

"Yeah?"

"What did you mean when you said 'life's funny even when it's not'?"

Pookie laughed softly. "Geeze, how do I explain?" She looked at the night sky, gathering her thoughts. "Dad always said that life's easier if you look for the things that make you smile more than the things that make you sad or mad. You know what he put in his will for Mom and me?"

"What?"

"A knock, knock joke."

"How's that?"

Pookie smiled. "Knock, knock."

"Who's there?"

"Me, always looking after my two best girls."

Tears appeared in Terry's eyes, and her hand covered her mouth. "That's absolutely beautiful."

"I imagine when he wrote it, he hoped we'd never read it, but I'm glad he wrote it. I still have it, pressed in my sketchbook."

"So that's what you meant about life being funny even when it's not?"

Pookie shook her head. "Not totally. Sometimes life isn't ha ha funny, but it's always funny as in odd, unpredictable, a mystery we'll never totally solve."

"I think I see that."

"When life gets tough, it's easier for me if I focus on the mystery more than any pain or sadness or anger. Do you see what I mean?"

"I think so." Terry smiled a sweet smile, a tender smile. She reached up and pushed a tendril of Pookie's blue hair away from Pookie's eyes. "You're a very special person, Pookie."

"So are you, Terry."

"I've never felt this comfortable with anyone this quickly."

Pookie leaned close. "Just meant to be. That's all."

First kiss on a staircase. There was no hurry to it. Pookie wasn't sure whether she started the kiss or if Terry did. It just happened, as natural as putting one foot in front of the other after making the decision to walk. There was more tenderness than passion to it, but it sealed a bond of the heart that would not likely be broken quickly nor easily.

The kiss ended abruptly as the door at the top of the stairs opened. Kathleen looked down on the pair, showing brief surprise at the embrace she interrupted.

"There you are," Kathleen said. "We were starting to wonder."

Judy peered over Kathleen's shoulder, looking toward the two young women as they sat on the stairs. "Pook, looks to me like you found a nice place for a romantic dinner."

Kathleen cleared her throat. "The party's about to break up. Why don't you come inside and help clean up?"

Kathleen turned and re-entered the room, but Judy reached into a back pocked and pulled out a pencil and a small pad of paper. She trotted down the stairs and handed them to Pookie.

"Just in case you need to write down phone numbers or emails or anything," Judy said. She turned and trotted up the stairs without waiting for an answer.

Terry smiled at Pookie. "Looks like your 'moms' approve."

Pookie didn't look up. She was too busy writing her email address and the number of the house phone at the ranch.

Chapter Ten

First Steps

The community house was full even without a potluck dinner to draw folks. Ted Rome, Dulson's city fire chief, stood at the front of the room, waiting for the conversation to settle as the people of the loosely knit Coldwater community greeted and visited with neighbors they usually only saw once every month or two.

The term neighbor means something different in a ranching community. The Kenton homestead was five miles from the Proctor place, but they were considered close neighbors, extension of family actually. Neighbors living twenty miles away still knew they were a part of Coldwater, and when they met up at the cattle auction, county fair, or the produce aisle at the grocery store, they greeted each other with a familiarity rarely found in any square block of a city suburb. Meetings at the Coldwater Community House offered a sense of belonging to people who largely lived a solitary existence centered around family, land, and livestock. Anyone driving through might laugh if they heard someone say they were in the Coldwater Community. Understandable considering all there was to be seen was a relatively small grain elevator and an old one-room schoolhouse saved from oblivion by conversion to a meeting place for a people who lived far and wide in sparsely populated ranching country. Unseen or not, the Coldwater Community lived with an intense sense of belonging for those who called it home. Never more so than when they had a shared mission, especially one as vital as a fire department.

Judy, Kathleen, and Pookie arrived before the crowd. To enter they used the front door key everybody knew was hidden under a rock by the step. Immediately, they begin setting up rows of folding chairs for a meeting instead of the usual tables and chairs used for the monthly potlucks. Kathleen started coffee, and Pookie set out cups, creamer, and sugar while Judy rummaged in the storeroom for the chalk and erasers left over from the days when the building had actually been a school.

I wonder if we could sell this at an antique store, Judy thought as she finally found chalk in an age-delicate cardboard box. She gently lifted the box to look on the bottom. Written there was "Binney and Smith, Co., Easton, Pennsylvania, 1910." Judy carefully placed the box back on the shelf and extracted a single piece of chalk, still intact after over a century. The box was half-full. She didn't think one more piece gone would matter. She found a slightly moth eaten eraser nearby and headed back into the main room with her treasures.

The three of them greeted Chief Rome when he arrived twenty minutes before the scheduled meeting time. It took all four of them to carry in heavy cardboard cartons he'd brought in the backseat of the Explorer that served as his command vehicle. He had them stack the boxes next to where he planned to stand. He cut the tape closing the top of the uppermost box. When Pookie tried to look inside, he put his hand over the box and said, "Later." Rome used the ancient but still useable chalkboard to write an agenda for the evening. There were only three items:

1. Election of officers and incorporation
2. Update on station construction and equipment
3. Training

At least thirty people filled the room, ten more than the usual potluck attendance. Kathleen used the same digital camera dedicated to illustrate articles. She snapped photos, capturing random shots, recording a historic moment for the people of Coldwater. The Kentons arrived, Harold still walking with a cane but standing proud, and they sat with Judy, Kathleen, and Pookie, the two households filling an entire row.

Chief Rome stood, but did not speak. The hum of multiple conversations continued all around him, but he stayed silent even as the minutes ticked past the scheduled starting time. He searched the room, his face expectant, as though he were waiting for something. After a time, Joe Bob Johnston stood from his front row seat and turned to face his neighbors. Conversation dwindled to a halt, as much from the power of his quiet presence as anything else.

"Well folks," Joe Bob said, his voice deep and gruff. "I guess you all know why we're here. That fire last spring damn near took one of our own home to Heaven, and we been lucky. That was the only one so far this year. The news says it's the worst fire season on record for the High Plains."

Harold stood, slowly. "I can't tell you all how grateful I am that the community has been so supportive of me and my family while I was in the hospital and while I've been recuperating. I--" Harold's voice trembled with emotion. He cleared his throat, "I now know just what fire can do. We got to have this fire department, for all our sakes."

Harold returned to his chair and Joe Bob turned to face Chief Rome.

"Chief, we're all grateful for your help. Without it, we'd be pretty lost. Do you mind getting this meeting going?" Joe Bob said as he returned to his own seat.

"I'm honored you've asked me to help you start a fire company. Truth is, for years, I've been asking the County to increase the number of rural departments. There's just too much country for the Dulson Fire Department to cover it all. I'm grateful to all of you for being willing to take on the job."

Joe Bob remained seated, but held above his head rolled blueprints. "Thanks to the Chief here, we already have our plans for a fire station. It's already been approved by the state fire marshal's office and the county commissioners. Bob Hanks, my boss, has set aside the money to build it. All we need is a fire company to staff it."

Chief Rome cleared his throat before speaking. "A fire station's worth nothing without firefighters, but we're getting ahead of ourselves. First step to start a company means we need officers. They'll be responsible for incorporating the company so that there is a legal entity we can use to authorize building of a fire station."

"What kind of officers?" Martha Kenton asked.

"A chief for sure and a deputy chief or a captain. You'll need at least one captain or lieutenant, and there has to be a secretary and treasurer."

"What about you, Harold? You'd make a fine

chief," a man at the back of room said.

Harold turned in his seat to look at the man. "Let me heal up enough to be a good ranch hand again before I go taking on firefighting."

"Amen to that," Martha said.

"You know, Judy and I were the ones with the idea of a fire department," Brad said.

Judy leaned close to him. "Hush up, will you? You're going to get us drafted into something big."

"No offense, Brad, but the chief might need to be someone with a few more birthdays than you. A young buck like you would be better as deputy chief or captain, the ones who actually do most of the hard work of fighting fire."

Pookie spoke in a clear voice, and the room went quiet. "Joe Bob, he's our chief." Joe Bob turned to look at the young woman, and she gazed directly at him, unwavering. "I'd trust you, and I'd follow you," she said.

"Young lady, I'm honored, but I don't know anything about firefighting," Joe Bob responded.

"None of us do," Judy said. "And Pookie's right. I've known you most of my life, and you got...well... wisdom. I'd follow you too."

"I nominate Joe Bob Johnston as chief," Curley Thompson called.

"I second," another man said.

Almost in unison, the entire room called, "Aye," and the new Coldwater Volunteer Fire Department had taken their first official action. Chief Rome turned the meeting over to a slightly stunned Joe Bob, and the other officers slipped into place with ease. Brad became deputy chief, Judy lieutenant, Kathleen treasurer, and Martha secretary. Chief Rome explained the process the officers must now undertake to incorporate the company and assured them he would be there to advise through the entire process. Joe Bob taped some of the blueprints to the blackboard, and there were a number of questions from ranchers and farmers experienced in the construction of barns and workshops. They learned in short order that fire stations had additional requirements, including water reservoirs, fire hydrants, and overhead plumping for rapid filling of fire truck reservoirs. The station would have bays for three trucks; Chief Rome advised them that they had already located a used Class A pumper the City of Lubbock was willing to loan to the company, and Texas State Forestry would donate a used fast attack wildland truck.

"As soon as we get you incorporated, you'll start getting your allocation from the state, and we can begin equipping your station with SCBAs, radios, bunker and wildland gear, and all the other things you'll need to fight fire," Chief Rome explained.

"What's an SCBA?" Judy asked.

"Self-Contained Breathing Apparatus," Rome answered.

Joe Bob looked at the blackboard, focusing on the last item on the agenda. He turned to Chief Rome. "Well, Ted, I may be chairing this meeting, but you have the answers. What do we need to do about training?"

Chief Rome opened the mysterious cardboard box and pulled out two heavy manuals. "If your officers agree, I've already gotten approval from the fire academy for me to supervise the training of your company to the standards for Firefighter I."

Joe Bob turned to the room at large. "Do I hear a motion?"

"So moved," Juanda Thompson said.

"And I second," Curley added. He grinned widely, obviously pleased with his role in making things happen.

A round of "Ayes," and a basic training plan was in place. Chief Rome passed out forms for those who wished to train, and as the forms were returned, he gave each one a copy of a training manual and a workbook.

Once everyone had settled back in their seats, Chief Rome turned back to the chalkboard and drew a triangle. Above the top corner, he wrote "Oxygen." On another corner, he wrote "Fuel," and on the third, he wrote "Heat."

"This is the fire triangle," Chief Rome said. "For you to have fire, all three elements must be present. Part of firefighting involves determining which of the three is easiest to remove. But the new texts talk about the fire tetrahedron."

"What the hell is a tetrahedron?" Curley asked.

"Something that's always looking for a tetra-*she*-dron," Brad responded. He looked to Judy. "Course I guess there could be two tetra-she-drons." He grunted only slightly as Judy's elbow dug into his rib cage.

Chief Rome sighed and twirled the chalk between his fingers. "I can tell you all have the makings of a fine fire company."

"Smart-alecks?" Brad asked.

"Humor," the Chief said. "It's the only thing that keeps you sane sometimes."

"Brad's always good for a laugh," Judy said.

"Or a groan," Kathleen added.

The chief used the chalk to mark a fourth dot on the board. He drew lines from the triangle to form an even pyramid – a tetrahedron. Beside the fourth point, he wrote *Chemical Reaction.* "It's possible to have all three of the components of fire, but it takes a chemical reaction to ignite them."

It was a start, but there was still so much to learn.

⁂

Judy wished they'd fed the horses before the meeting. It was dark when they pulled into the yard. Judy dropped Kathleen off at the house, and Pookie stayed with her in the truck as Judy drove across the yard toward the corrals. Judy left the truck running and the headlights on, illuminating the small haystack beside the pens. As they walked toward the hay, a strange sound disrupted the night, a buzz that jarred the nerves.

"What's that?" Pookie asked.

Judy's answer was to grab the young woman by the back of her shirt to pull her unceremoniously toward the running truck.

"What the hey!" Pookie demanded.

Judy pulled a flashlight from the pocket on the driver's side door, and used the light to search the ground near the hay.

"There it is," Judy said.

Caught in the beam of light, a prairie rattler buzzed angrily.

"Jesus! I nearly stepped on it," Pookie said.

"Glad you didn't," Judy said. She reached inside the pickup cab once again, opening a pocket on the front of the seat cover and extracting a pump-action .410 shotgun. "Here, hold the light and shine it on the snake," Judy said, handing Pookie the flashlight. She pumped a shell into the chamber and sent the snake to rattler heaven. Inside the corrals, the horses snorted and shied.

The light waivered as Pookie's hand shook.

"That was really loud," Pookie said.

"A four-ten is the smallest of the shotguns, but all shotguns are pretty loud," Judy responded.

Pookie stared at the snake, mesmerized. "Would I have died if it bit me?"

"Maybe…for sure you would have been darned sick and maybe lost a foot or a leg."

"I've…I've never seen anything shot before. I don't like guns much."

"Pook, if I see a rattler out in the pasture, I leave it, but we can't have them around the barn. If they den up here, it's a constant threat to the livestock and us. We'll start looking for a bull snake to turn loose in the barn. They keep the rattlers away."

"I…I know rattlesnakes are dangerous, but I just don't like guns much. Had no idea that was in your truck."

"I keep the chamber empty so it's safer for traveling. It's the same one dad kept in his truck. Never been used on anything but a rattlesnake." Judy took off her hat and scratched her head. "Pookie, if you're going to live on a ranch, you at least need to know enough about firearms to be safe. Tomorrow…tomorrow I'd like to teach you some basics, mainly safety."

They both turned toward the house as they heard the back door open.

"You two okay?" Kathleen yelled.

"Just fine, honey. I shot a rattlesnake," Judy answered.

In the dark, they heard the back door open and

close as Kathleen went back inside.

Pookie pulled her gaze from the snake and looked at Judy. "Okay, you can teach me." She looked at the snake. "If I see one of those again, I have to know what to do."

"That's a girl. Now, would you get a shovel out of the back of the truck? Even dead, that snake's still dangerous. We need to bury it."

Judy put the shotgun back in the truck and Pookie went for the shovel.

Chapter Eleven

New Developments

Pookie's black motorcycle boots were somewhat worse for wear since beginning her new career as a cowhand. She scrubbed every bit of cow and horse manure from every nook and cranny on the boots then applied a thick layer of polish and rubbed until the leather surface was as mirror shiny. She could have used the boots as the reflective surface as she applied makeup. She could have but didn't. Instead, she disappeared for nearly two hours into the guest bathroom, scrubbing herself as thoroughly as she'd scrubbed her boots, and then re-bluing her hair and applying her full contingent of makeup, including black eyeliner and lipstick, items she had not used since her arrival on the Proctor Ranch.

"What the hell is she doing in there?" Judy asked, looking up from the re-run of *Gunsmoke* she and Kathleen were watching to pass the time as they awaited the arrival of their guests.

Kathleen laughed and snuggled closer to Judy on the loveseat. "What do you think she's doing? Have you forgotten that Terry Morris is coming with April and Sophia?"

"I know she likes the girl, but dang, Terry won't be impressed if Pookie scrubs off all her skin."

"Hmmmmm, seems like I remember some well-polished boots and freshly starched shirt and jeans the first time we went out to dinner," Kathleen responded.

Judy laughed and kissed Kathleen on the top of her head. "That's true. I even dug out some of the old makeup I used when I worked in the city."

"You did?" Kathleen said, surprised. "I'm sorry, honey. I couldn't tell."

"That's because it had all dried up or turned to dust. It went in the trash."

Kathleen's laugh was deep in her throat. "That's okay, sweetheart. I was already in love with you. Mascara wouldn't have made a bit of difference."

"I saw it on you, but it didn't matter. I was already drowning in those brown eyes of yours."

The kiss was long and slow. As it continued, they shifted positions, miraculously increasing the intimacy of their already cozy embrace. When Kathleen unsnapped the top two snaps of Judy's western shirt, her hand slipped comfortably inside shirt and bra, teasing at an already erect nipple. Judy moaned softly, reluctantly ending the kiss.

"Honey, we got company coming," Judy said.

"If they delay long enough, they won't be the only ones coming," Kathleen answered huskily.

That's when they heard the bathroom door open. Kathleen hastily pulled her hand from Judy's shirt, and they worked together, franticly refastening the shirt, having time for only one snap before Pookie walked into the living room, wearing the terry-cloth bathrobe that was a hand-me-down from Kathleen. The two women remained snuggling on the loveseat, but there was a subtle change in position, a less intimate feel, one more appropriate for the presence of their young housemate.

"What time did they say they'd be here?" Pookie asked.

"About three," Kathleen answered.

Pookie looked at the old-fashioned clock ticking on the wall. The short hand was on two and the long hand at the quarter-hour. "I better hurry." She looked down at her lesbian moms. "And you two don't have time for that," she said, pointing at Judy's shirt where the top snap on the right side was attached to the second snap on the left side. Pookie turned and walked rapidly up the stairs to her room.

Judy blushed crimson. "Well, I guess she knows what we were doing."

Kathleen laughed so hard she nearly rolled off the loveseat. Judy caught her, holding her in place before she hit the floor.

"Does this mean I can wear the 'Boobies make me smile' shirt around her now?" Judy asked.

Kathleen wiped at laughter-induced tears. "Yes, honey. I think she can handle it," Kathleen responded.

The couple remained snuggled, but their attention returned to the witty repartee between Doc and Chester on the TV screen. The sound was low, offering more of a distraction as they waited than any serious entertainment. When Pookie returned to the living room, she was perfectly tricked out in punk high dress. The studs on her dog collar were freshly polished, and black designer jeans with perfectly positioned wear-holes on the legs, black leggings showing beneath, replaced the blue denim jeans she adopted for ranch work. Her black t-shirt was one Judy had never seen before, the name of a band Judy had never heard emblazoned over her right breast.

"You look great, Pook," Kathleen said.

"Do you think…will she…?"

"You'll knock her socks off," Judy said.

Pookie sat poised on the edge of the couch. She picked up a copy of the *Dulson County Reporter* from the coffee table and began tearing little chunks off one corner.

"Now, don't you go leaving a pile of trash on the couch. We cleaned this whole place, remember," Kathleen said.

Pookie put the newspaper back on the table, and gathered her little pile of paper bits, carrying them to the trashcan in the kitchen. While there, she looked out the window down the county road by the house.

"Are you sure they know the way?" Pookie asked.

"Pook, April travels all over the Panhandle for her newspaper. She knows the way to Dulson and Highway 84 north. You can't miss the turn onto CR 10 at the grain elevator. I'm sure they'll find us," Judy said.

"I hope they're not late," Pookie said, still staring down the road.

"If you don't settle down, I'll be tempted to give you one of those tranquilizers the vet gave us for Useless so she won't puke when we take her in for her shots," Judy said.

Kathleen shifted from her position on the loveseat and stood. "Come on, Pookie. Let's stuff some of those jalapeños."

"That's a good idea," Judy said. "Everyone loved those at the Ladies' Room."

Pookie looked down at her perfectly placed outfit. "But I'm all dressed."

"You can wear an apron," Kathleen said.

"Wait!" Judy said, following Kathleen into the

kitchen. "Maybe jalapeños aren't the best idea."

Kathleen looked puzzled. "Why?"

"They can be too hot for some folks," Judy said.

"You know good and well that the cheese mixture I use mellows them out so there's just a little bite."

Judy shifted from one foot to the other, until she finally pulled Kathleen close and whispered into Kathleen's ear. "What if we want to finish what we started after we go to bed tonight?"

"So?"

Judy gazed pointedly into Kathleen's eyes. "Remember the last time?"

Kathleen's eyes widened. "Ohhhh…" She reached into a drawer and pulled out a box of latex gloves she kept for cleaning. "Here, Pookie. We better use these," she said as she pulled a pair from the box and handed them to the younger woman.

"Where's my pair?" Judy asked.

Kathleen swatted Judy playfully on the behind. "Go watch *Gunsmoke*. Stuffed jalapeños are Pookie's and my specialty."

Judy gratefully obeyed, leaving the kitchen for the living room. As they worked, Kathleen and Pookie heard the television volume increase slightly. Judy really did like the old Western.

⁂

Pookie wiped sweaty palms against the legs of her jeans. Sketches, paintings, and small clay sculptures covered the drawing board, the desk top, the futon, and even the floor. For such a young artist, Pookie had an impressive portfolio. She had been so relieved when her mother agreed to ship all of her art she had to her new home in Texas. Judy and Kathleen moved furniture in the office/studio they all shared and emptied a closet so that there was a place for Pookie's collection. Now, feeling as though she were exposing her very soul, Pookie showed it all to Terry.

Terry stood, moving only slightly in tight little circles so that she could take in the panorama of art surrounding her. Her face showed only surprise, her mouth hanging slightly open. For the longest time, she said nothing.

"I'm...I'm sorry there weren't enough horses for us to all go riding at once," Pookie said, fidgeting nervously at a loose thread on the strategically worn holes in her jeans.

"I'm not." Terry stood straight, appearing to rein in the amazement that left her speechless. "Pookie, you are an amazing artist."

The usually unflappable Pookie blushed. "You really think so?"

Terry sighed, shaking her head, her mouth working soundlessly as she sought words for her feelings. "Pookie...I...I can't tell you how moved I am by your art." She gazed directly into Pookie's face, her expression intensifying. "How moved I am by you."

Terry reached for Pookie's hand and raised her from where she sat in an office chair. As she stepped closer, Terry wrapped her arms around Pookie, holding her close. They stood in a long, slow embrace. Respiration for both women became rapid and shaky. In time, Pookie leaned back to look into Terry's eyes and then gently touch her fingers along the side of Terry's face. The kiss was long and slow, growing in intensity as the young women used tongues and lips to explore the intimate interior of the other's mouth.

The passion became so intense that Terry's knees weakened, and Pookie wrapped her arms ever more tightly around Terry as she felt the other sway. Pookie guided Terry gently to a seat in the office chair and then turned to gather the eleven-by-seventeen mixed media depictions of the sculpture she and Judy were creating from where they stood upright against the futon back. She placed the art carefully behind a filing cabinet and then took Terry's hand to pull her softly toward a seat beside her on the futon.

Making out is such a coarse term, hardly accurate to describe the gentle intensity with which Pookie and Terry kissed and as their hands and mouths became bold in where they touched and tasted. Terry moaned as Pookie nibbled and licked at the gentle curve where neck met shoulder.

"You are so different from Marilyn," Terry said, breathlessly.

Pookie stopped what she was doing, but kept her body intimately close to the woman beside her. "Marilyn…your lover who…who…?"

"Who killed herself, yes."

"How am I different?" Pookie asked.

"You're bold and brazen, not caring what people think. Maybe because of that, everyone seems to love you."

Pookie laughed without humor. "Not my stepfather."

"Then he's a fool."

"Well, yeah. That's a given," Pookie said.

Terry laughed. "See. That's what I mean. Marilyn…Marilyn was so afraid, cared so much about what her parents, the preacher, people in the church —heck, even God—she cared so much what others thought of her."

"I was lucky. My dad taught me when I was little not to be afraid to be me," Pookie said.

"How did he die?"

"Car wreck on an icy road. He had a job to deliver in Castle Rock. I wanted to go with him, but he wouldn't let me because the weather was bad."

"I'm so sorry," Pookie.

Pookie pulled away, leaning forward, her elbows on her knees. "I grieve sometimes still, but then I remember, at least I had him for a time. If I hadn't had that, I wouldn't even know that I was supposed to grieve the best dad in the world." She turned to look at Terry. "That would be a whole lot worse."

Terry used her right hand to trace random patterns gently on Pookie's back. "Yes, it would."

"So, I'm a lot different from Marilyn. What about your other lovers? Am I all that different?"

Terry sat perfectly still. She turned her face to look out the window. "I...I haven't had any other lovers."

Pookie took Terry's hand in her own. "You know, you don't have to stop grieving to get on with your life," she said.

Terry put her hand on Pookie's arm and pulled her back into a close embrace. "You know, I'm learning that. I met this amazing girl, and she is teaching me so much."

They kissed again with renewed passion.

"Pookie." Terry said her mouth close to Pookie's ear.

"Yes?"

"Why don't you show me your room?"

Pookie leaned back, surprised. The surprise

evaporated quickly, replaced by a mischievous smile.

"It would be my pleasure," Pookie responded.

"But," Terry looked out the window intently. "What if they come back while we…?"

"Don't worry," Pookie said. "Judy said she was going to take them to the spring in Duran Canyon. I've been there, and even when we rode pretty hard, it was over a two-hour ride. Since April and Sophia aren't experienced riders, they'll take it slow, and Kathleen will want to gather some watercress at the spring. We have time."

❧❧❧❧

Kathleen poured four huge tumblers of sweetened iced tea as April and Sophia walked a tad unsteadily through the back service porch and into the kitchen. They each gratefully accepted a glass and downed much of the contents in rapid gulps.

"I didn't realize riding could be such thirsty work," Kathleen said.

"The sugar's good for you too. We expended a lot of energy on that ride," Judy said as she followed her guests into the room and accepted her own tumbler of tea from Kathleen.

Sophia and April moved to take seats around the kitchen table, each lowering herself slowly to the chair.

Kathleen laughed as she watched. "It does take a little time for the body to adjust to time in the saddle," she said.

"I'll admit I'm a little sore," Sophia said.

"A little sore, and the world looks just a little funny to me," April said, confusion in her tone.

"I still get that, even though I've ridden all my

life. After a while, your body adjusts to the different height and balance that comes with being on a horse. My guess is it's a little like getting your land legs back after being at sea," Judy said.

"That makes sense," April responded.

Sophia shifted uncomfortably in her chair.

"You two can help yourselves to the Jacuzzi tub in the master bedroom for a nice soak, and I have some salve that's good for saddle sores if you need it," Judy said.

"For people or for horses?" April asked.

"Yes," Judy answered.

Sophia smiled as she looked toward Judy and Kathleen. "Thank you so much for that wonderful experience. I had never ridden except short rides when I was a girl visiting a friend who had a pony, and renting a horse for an hour's ride in New Mexico."

Kathleen moved to the sink and emptied a shopping bag full of watercress into the sink. She began a thorough washing of the wild salad.

"I've never eating wild…what did you call it?" April asked.

"Watercress," Kathleen answered.

Sophia breathed deeply, closing her eyes to enjoy the scent. "What is that wonderful smell?"

Judy walked to where the crock-pot simmered on the counter, lifting the lid. "It's some of Kathleen's famous Irish stew."

"Honey, the ladies would probably like a snack. Would you get the jalapeño poppers out of the refrigerator?" Kathleen asked.

Judy pulled the plastic container filled with stuffed peppers out of the refrigerator, removed the lid, and took one from the top layer before setting the bowl on the table in front of their guests.

"I remember these from the potluck," April said.

"Me too," Sophia said, as she took her own pepper from the bowl.

Kathleen retrieved small plates and paper napkins from the cupboard, setting them on the table. "Forgive Judy. Sometimes she forgets that people like to be civilized when they eat." She gave Judy a loving tug on her ear.

"What can I say? I've eaten too many meals out of a saddle bag or sitting on a tailgate," Judy said. She paused, looking around. "Hey! Wonder where the girls are?"

"That's right. I didn't see them outside, but maybe they went for a walk." Kathleen grasped the cabinet door she'd left open after taking plates from a shelf. She swung it closed, making a sound loud enough to be heard throughout the house.

All four women heard a thump from the floor above.

"Uhhhh…that's from Pookie's room," Judy said.

The muffled sounds of scurrying could be heard above, followed shortly by the "thump, thump" of someone hurrying down the stairs. Terry appeared in the doorway, looking artificially nonchalant.

"So, did you all have a good ride?" she asked.

None of the older women answered. They sat in silence, each wondering if they should tell Terry that her shirt was inside out.

"Yes, we…uh…had a great ride," April said.

"The spring was beautiful," Sophia added.

Pookie followed Terry at a somewhat more relaxed pace. She appeared in the doorway, stepping directly into the kitchen. "Oh great, the poppers are out." She took two from the bowl, one in each hand. As she ate one, she took the other to Terry and raised it toward her lips. Although she blushed, Terry smiled as she ate directly from Pookie's hand. Pookie glanced at Terry's attire, then leaned close to whisper in Terry's ear.

Terry made a noise very similar to the sound of a strangling cat and rushed out of the room and back up the stairs. Pookie returned to the table, placed four poppers on a plate, and then picked it up along with a handful of napkins.

"I better go see if I can help," Pookie said as she left the kitchen and followed Terry up the stairs.

The kitchen was painfully silent for a moment.

"Kathleen, honey, I don't think we need to make up the futon in the office tonight," Judy said.

April was the first to laugh. The others followed.

Chapter Twelve

Godsend?

Joe Bob spread the plans for the new fire station on the folding table where all the Coldwater Volunteer Fire Department officers now gathered. As chief, Joe Bob had followed the precedent established by Ted Rome when he chaired the organizational meeting. The agenda was written on the black board. There were three items:

1. Fire station
2. Stuff from the County
3. What's next?

"Well heck, Joe Bob, I can understand the basic schematics for the building, but there's a bunch of stuff here I just don't understand," Brad said.

Judy traced a finger along a series of lines, apparently water pipes, that ran along the top of the equipment bays. "Why the heck they got plumbing up on the ceiling?"

"Damned if I know," Joe Bob responded.

"Wait," Judy picked up the blueprints, studying up one small segment. "Here it is. Ohhh, that makes sense."

"Well then, explain to the rest of us," Brad said.

"They have huge spigots right over the trucks. I bet it's so you can fill the tanks without having to move the trucks."

Joe Bob pointed at the designation for propane heating units suspended from the ceiling at all four corners. "Be handy in the winter. Plumbing won't freeze like outside water supplies."

Everyone looked toward Kathleen as she let out a low whistle. She sat at a separate table, looking through the budget and accounting forms Joe Bob had picked up from the County Manager. As treasurer, she was the one tasked with interpreting the financial bureaucrat quagmire.

"What's up?" Judy asked.

"When we get our station built and the two trucks Ted Rome arranged for us, we'll qualify as a 'sub-station.' Do you know how much we'll get from the state every year just for operation?"

"How much?" Martha asked. She sat beside Kathleen, taking notes for the minutes.

"We'll receive $120,000 from the state fire fund."

"And that's not all," Joe Bob said. "When I went by to pick up our paperwork, the County Manager sat me down to talk about the grants we need to apply for so we can start buying trucks and equipment. There's state money and FEMA money through the Assistance to Firefighter Grant and some other programs. He said we need to get a new Class A pumper as soon as possible and said it would be at least a quarter million dollars."

"Holy crap! That's even worse than a new combine," Brad said.

"You're telling me," Joe Bob responded. He tugged at his mustache and looked into the faces of his officers. "Folks, we've taken on a big job here."

Martha's lips lightened into a thin line. Angrily,

she set her pencil down on her note pad. "And it's worth every nickel—our money, state money, federal money—if it will keep one person from going through what my Harold went through."

The room went silent, heavy with the weight of Martha's words.

"Won't argue with you one bit, Martha," Joe Bob said, breaking the silence.

"None of us would. You are totally right," Judy added. Kathleen simply put her arm around Martha's shoulders, saying nothing.

"Mama, we're all in this one hundred percent," Brad said.

Joe Bob came around the table and took a chair at the head, letting go of the blueprint. All on its own, the paper rolled into a tube shape, ready to be stored.

"None of us doubt we need to do this. It's just a little intimidating." Joe Bob picked up a paper on the top of the stack he'd left at his chair. It was a required equipment list. "Thank God Ted Rome is going to supervise training. Hell, I'm chief, and I don't even remember what an SCBA is."

Judy opened her Firefighter I textbook to the index in the back. "Self-Contained Breathing Apparatus," she said.

"Guess that's those air tanks and masks that make you sound like Darth Vader," Brad said.

"Think you're right, Brad. We'll all be learning how to use those," Joe Bob said.

Martha was taking notes again, her anger dissipated. "Just take it one step at a time, one step at a time," she said.

"Speaking of which, what's our next step, Chief?" Kathleen asked.

Joe Bob shook his head slowly. "I'm still just Joe Bob, Miss Kathleen. Don't call me Chief until I've proven I can do the job." He shuffled through his stack of papers, retrieving some hand-written notes. "But I can answer your question. Kathleen, you need to go meet with Sue Bradshaw, one of the deputies in the County Treasurer's office. She'll be teaching you about how the accounting is handled. The County has already put out a call for bids to build the station and my boss has arranged to make payments directly to the County to pay for it. He didn't even break a sweat when I told him the price." Joe Bob looked through his notes, squinting slightly at his own handwriting. "As you all know Ted Rome will be here at the Community Center every Tuesday evening starting at seven p.m. to start our training, and we had twenty people sign up as trainees." Joe Bob paused, scratching at the lip beneath his heavy mustache. "Martha, as secretary, you need to get with Ted, and he'll start teaching you about signing up for something called NFIRS."

"What's that?" Brad asked.

"Well, hell, Brad. You had to ask. Ted told me what it stood for, but darned if I remember."

"National Fire Incident Reporting System," said a voice from the back of the room, surprising them all.

Every head turned to face a man standing just inside the still open doorway. He was tall with shaggy hair and just a little grizzled looking. He wore a passably clean t-shirt, jeans, and heavy lace-up boots. A manila folder rested in his right hand.

"Good evening," Joe Bob said. "Who might you be, sir?"

The man walked directly to Joe Bob and offered his hand for a handshake. "Name's Donald Guyette;

most folks call me Guy. I'm doing some work in the area, and I'm renting the house on the old Valdez place."

Martha looked at the man sternly. "News travels fast around here, and I hadn't heard anyone was moving into that house."

"I was getting ready to rent a place in town, then I heard you all were starting a new fire company." He opened the manila folder and placed it in front of Joe Bob. "I've been a firefighter for over twenty-five years, including being a State Forestry crew boss for wildland crews and an officer, including chief, for three different companies. You'll see here a list of some of my qualifications."

Martha, Brad, and Judy all took positions standing behind Joe Bob, striving to read the list.

"What's ICS?" Brad asked.

"Incident Command System. It's what rules all emergency service systems from local fire right up to massive FEMA responses to natural disasters. I'm qualified up to ICS 400 for Command and General Staff." The man nodded toward the paper. "As you can see, I'm certified for Firefighter I and II and have completed the Texas Fire Academy officer training. I'm fully certified in all levels of HazMat too."

"HazMat?" Martha asked.

"Hazardous Materials," the man answered.

Joe Bob chuckled softly. "Mr....what was your name again?"

"Guy, just call me Guy."

"Well sir, I do believe you're a godsend."

"No offense, Joe Bob, but are you dead set on being chief?" Brad asked.

"I'd sure as hell feel a whole lot better as captain

and Guy here as chief," Joe Bob answered.

"So moved," Brad said.

"Second," Martha called.

In the chorus of "ayes" that followed, no one seemed to notice that Judy said nothing. It was just an itch on the back of her neck, not enough to make her want to speak up but enough…enough to make her uneasy.

❧❧❧❧❧

Pookie met Judy and Kathleen in the kitchen when they returned home from the fire officer's meeting. The light was still on in the den/studio they all shared, and an Ebony drawing pencil was tucked behind her right ear.

"How'd it go?" Pookie asked.

"You won't believe what happened," Kathleen said.

"What?"

"A man just moved into Coldwater who is a super qualified firefighter and fire officer. He blew us away with all his qualifications. Joe Bob took the job of captain, and we elected the new guy as chief."

"That's cool," Pookie said. She looked at Judy's face. "Isn't it?"

"I think so," Judy said. "It just happened so fast. I wonder if we shouldn't have taken a little more time to get to know the man."

"His qualifications were pretty hard to doubt," Kathleen said. She looked quizzically at Judy. "If you had doubts, why didn't you speak up? I thought you were awfully quiet driving home."

"Well, it sure seemed like a no-brainer but…I

don't know, it just felt a little funny," Judy said.

Kathleen chewed at her lower lip. "Well, if your funny feeling turns out right, if we voted him in, we can vote him out."

"Yeah, I'm sure you're right." Judy took a glass from the cabinet and retrieved ice and sweet tea from the refrigerator. "How was your evening?" she asked Pookie.

"Great! I got some sketches done, but…I thought of something."

"Yes?" Judy asked.

Pookie turned to Kathleen. "Are you still going to town tomorrow?"

"I think so. You want to come?"

"Yes," Pookie said. "I'd…I'd like to get a long distance card."

Judy stopped mid-drink and lowered her glass. "Oh heck, I nearly forgot." Judy set her glass on the counter and left the kitchen abruptly, heading toward the master bedroom.

"What's that about?" Pookie asked Kathleen.

Kathleen's face shone with a mischievous smile. "You'll see."

Judy came back, a smart phone in her hand. "Here you go, Pookie. We got this for you yesterday, and I've had it charging so you wouldn't have to wait to use it. We just added another phone to our family plan. You have unlimited calling and text."

Pookie stared at the phone, a shocked expression on her face.

"Go ahead, take it, Pook," Kathleen said.

"We thought…well…we figured you'd need to be making some regular calls to Amber now."

Pookie blinked back tears, taking the phone, her

hand shaking slightly. Judy handed her a piece of paper with a number written on it.

"That's your new number," Kathleen said. She looked at the kitchen clock. "It's not too late, why don't you go call her?"

Pookie jumped up, hugging Judy around the neck. The disparity in the height of the woman and the girl meant Pookie's feet dangled freely in the air.

"You guys are the best," Pookie called before dropping to the ground and wrapping her arms around Kathleen's waist. It was a brief hug. She was up the stairs and in her room before Judy had time to retrieve her half-empty tea glass from the counter.

Chapter Thirteen

Fast Track

The concrete slab was laid before anybody even realized what was happening.

Judy picked up the phone on the third ring. Kathleen and Pookie sat at the dinner table, their meals half-eaten. They looked anxiously at Judy as she hit the "talk" button on the phone.

"Proctor Ranch, Judy Proctor speaking," Judy answered. Pause. She looked at Kathleen and Pookie and silently mouthed the name "Joe Bob," as she listened. "What? No, I haven't been down to the community building today." Pause. "What? But the County just put it out for bids. How could they have started construction on the fire station?" Pause. "Hold on." Judy put the phone to her shoulder and looked at Kathleen.

"Did Guy Guyette turn in his membership paperwork to you?"

"No, but maybe to Martha since she's secretary," Kathleen responded.

"Joe Bob said he already checked with her and Brad. Nobody has his membership application, and no one has a phone number for him."

"What's this about the fire station?" Kathleen asked.

Judy lifted the phone back to her face. "Joe Bob,

we don't have paperwork or a phone number for Guy. I don't think there's much we can do before morning when the county offices open, and Kathleen and Pookie are dying to hear what's happening." Pause. "Want me to go with you?" Pause. "Okay, I should be done with chores by 8:30. Pick me up on your way to town?" Pause. "See you then. Good night."

Judy hit the "end" button and faced her lover and ward. "Holy shit!" she said.

"Holy shit what?" Kathleen said, an edge to her voice.

"Joe Bob drove by the community building, and there was a crew working there. They'd just finished pouring the slab for the fire station, and all the materials for a full metal building are already stacked, ready for construction."

"That's not possible. Ted Rome said the County has just barely put it out for bid."

Judy picked at the roast chicken on her plate, suddenly uninterested in food. "Joe Bob said he stopped and asked the crew boss what the hell he was doing. It's some company from Abilene that specializes in building fire stations. The man said Guy Guyette hired them."

"But...but the bids?" Kathleen said.

"The crew boss told Joe Bob that they are authorized as a vendor through the state and they don't have to do a bid."

"Can that be right?"

"Damned if I know. Joe Bob and I are going to town in the morning. We'll look up Ted Rome and the County Clerk. They should have some answers."

Pookie slammed her fork flat onto the table. "Asshole!"

"Pookie?" Kathleen said.

"It doesn't fucking matter if they don't have to do bids. This fire company doesn't belong to that Guy fellow. It belongs to us, the people who live here."

Judy and Kathleen sat in stunned silence, broken only when Judy laughed, with more resignation than humor. "As usual, Pookie girl, you managed to go right to the heart of things and say it all."

"Fuck," Kathleen said.

"Well, that pretty well sums it up as well," Judy agreed.

❧❧❧❧

Judy and Joe Bob sat in worn out chairs that Judy remembered as surplus from the old junior high school. A tear in the plastic seat-cover kept catching on the back of her jeans when she moved. Judy figured the Dulson Fire Department preferred to invest money in fire equipment rather than office furniture. Outside the office, Judy could hear Dulson firefighters work as they performed maintenance on the engines in the bays.

"What do you mean there's nothing we can do?" Joe Bob asked.

Ted Rome's desk chair squeaked as he leaned back, a look of frustration on his face. "Not for now, at least. When you all elected Guy Guyette chief, it was a bad time. You don't have bylaws for your company yet so he can make up the rules as he goes."

"But what about bids for the fire station?" Judy asked.

Ted scratched his chin. "The County Treasurer is mad as hops, and the County Attorney is doing some research, but I called the State Fire Marshall's Office. Turns out that Abilene company really is approved as a state vendor for station construction. It's a tad iffy, but the station may be finished by the time the County Attorney gives an official opinion."

"Can't we file a restraining order or something?" Joe Bob asked.

"Joe Bob, you all voted him in as chief. He's already registered himself as the sole representative of the company with NFIRS. The only way to stop him is to vote him out. Do you think you can do that?"

"I don't know," Joe Bob answered. "Most of the ones who signed up to train as firefighters are the young men out in Coldwater. Tad Romig's wife told me Guy had already been to their house, bragging on how Tad was going to make a fine firefighter and giving him a t-shirt and hat from some of the fire equipment companies. She sounded disgusted, but she said Tad ate it up with a spoon. Then there's Brad Kenton..."

"Oh God, no," Judy said. "Don't tell me. Love Brad like a brother, but it doesn't take much for him to start thinking with his ego."

"When I called last night to ask Brad if he knew about the crew building the station, he sounded proud as punch that Guy had told him and none of the other officers," Joe Bob said.

Judy moaned and Ted nervously clicked away with the ballpoint pen he'd taken from his pocket.

"I'm a damn fool," Joe Bob said.

"You're not alone. All of us officers voted for him. We were half-scared to death that night when we saw everything we had to do and realized just how little we knew. Guy walked in looking like a superhero," Judy said.

"You're kind, Miss Judy, but I noticed even if the others didn't. When we all voted 'aye,' you didn't say anything."

Judy shook her head. "That's exactly right. I didn't say anything. My silence was a vote for him the same as if I'd shouted it out loud."

Ted threw the belabored pen on his desk. "Near as I can tell, you all aren't alone. The State Fire Marshall's office gave me the names of two other fire companies Guy started here in Texas. Seems like he likes starting fire stations, but he only stays six to nine months. I called the chief at one of the companies."

"What did he say?" Joe Bob asked.

"Said that Guy knows what he's doing. He got them the best equipment for the money and set their systems up right."

"Can't say that I'm happy to hear that," Judy said.

"It wasn't all compliments," Ted continued. "The man said Guy nearly tore their new company apart, and he said something that really worried me."

"What's that?"

"He asked if Coldwater had any women firefighters," Ted said.

"Yes?" Judy asked. "What about it?"

"The man said to be careful, watch out for your women. He said Guy's the worst woman hater he's ever seen."

Joe Bob's face turned red, and Judy sat up straight.

"Won't be the first time I've dealt with an asshole," Judy said.

There was a fiery glint in his eye when Joe Bob turned to face her. "Just know you won't be standing alone, not you nor Kathleen nor Martha nor Pookie. I got your back, just as much as I can. I got your back."

"I know, Joe Bob. I know."

✽ ✽ ✽ ✽

Judy, Kathleen, and Pookie stepped out of Judy's truck and looked with awe at the nearly completed infrastructure for the new fire station. It had been less than week since the Abilene crew started work and the walls were already up. The bay doors were not installed yet, and they could see inside to see that plumbing and electrical conduit were already in place. What's more, sitting inside the half-finished station were two trucks, a Class A pumper and a rapid attack brush truck. Judy recognized both types from the reading she had already completed in her *Essentials of Firefighting* manual.

"Where did the trucks come from?" Pookie asked.

"The pumper's on loan," Guy's voice boomed from behind them, startling all three women. He smiled, apparently pleased at their reaction. "The brush truck is a gift from State Forestry."

Judy turned toward Guy. He stepped so close she could smell salami on his breath, and he towered over her, his expression just shy of a leer. He poked so hard at the textbook and task book Judy held under her arm that he nearly knocked them from her grasp.

"You won't need those tonight," he said. "We're going to train on the trucks. If we have a fire while we're teaching all you rookies, you at least need to be able to run the pumps and nozzles. But that's for the firefighters. Why don't you ladies go inside the community building and make some coffee or something?"

Judy opened the door to her truck, forcing Guy

to take a step back. She put her books on the rear seat. Pookie and Kathleen stepped close to her, handing Judy their books as well. In the process, the force of three women caused Guy to take another step backward.

"I'm a lieutenant in this company," Judy said. "I'll train on the trucks."

"Trucks for me too," Pookie said.

"I'll go for the trucks too," Kathleen said.

Guy opened his mouth to say something, but he stopped. Judy looked him full in the face, and she was shocked at what she saw – fear. The big man was terrified.

"Hey Judy, get over here," Brad called from just inside a bay door. "You have to see this."

The three women left the erstwhile chief standing and walked toward the station. Once inside, Brad gave them a tour of the half-finished station and the trucks, as proud as a child showing visiting grandparents every toy in the toy box. As Brad gave them a personal tour, other members of the company arrived for the Tuesday night training. Brad's tour group grew with each new arrival. Guy watched from a relative distance.

Ted Rome pulled into the field that served as a parking area beside the station and got out of the old Explorer that was the Dulson Fire Department command vehicle. As he walked toward the station, Guy moved into action. He moved toward Brad's informal tour group, stepping between Ted and the fledgling firefighters.

"Brad, pull the pumper onto the apron," Guy called.

Brad turned to grin at Judy and her two companions. "Come on," he said. "There's room for four in the cab. You all can ride with me."

The three women were almost as excited as Brad at the new—to them anyway—trucks, and they happily climbed inside. As they took seats in the truck, with Brad in the driver's seat, they studied the strange configuration of the seats.

"What's this attached to the seat?" Kathleen asked.

"They're SCBAs – the air tanks," Brad answered. "They're set up so that firefighters can be geared up and ready to go as soon as you get to a fire."

"Should we do it?" Pookie asked.

"Not on your life," Brad answered. "I tried earlier and damn near couldn't get out of the truck. I haven't figured out the trick to the release latch. We better let Guy or Ted show us how."

"But you know how to drive the truck, right?" Judy asked.

"Do I know how to drive the truck?" Brad responded derisively. He turned the key in the ignition. Nothing happened. Ted stepped onto the running board and Brad rolled down the window.

"Did you remember to turn on the battery kill switch?" Ted asked.

"The what?" Brad responded.

Ted opened the driver's door and directed Brad's attention to a large toggle switch beside the seat. "You can't afford to have a dead battery on a fire truck," Ted said. "Most are equipped with two batteries plus a switch on the driver's side in the cab that totally disconnects the batteries so there is no drain if the truck isn't driven for a few days."

Ted clicked the switch to the on position. Brad hit the ignition switch and the engine roared to life.

Brad blushed. "Guy didn't tell me about the kill

switch," he said.

"Riiiiiight," Judy responded. Pookie stifled a giggle.

Judy watched as Brad pulled the truck forward. The basic operation was easy, simpler than the four-ton tandem axel trucks she'd driven when helping local harvest crews. The mystery came in trying to understand the buttons, lights, and switches across the dashboard. She assumed it was for operation of radio, lights, and sirens, and the pump mechanism. Judy felt like an astronaut studying the controls of a space shuttle.

Once both trucks were parked outside the building, Guy drove the brush truck, the real training began. Everyone watched as Ted and a Dulson firefighter he'd brought along pulled hose from a compartment marked "Preset 1." They fully extended the hose, laying it beside the truck, the firefighter staying with the nozzle. Ted quickly organized the trainees into groups of four or five, and Ted supervised training on the pumper for one group while Guy did the same for another group on the brush truck. The Dulson firefighter worked with another team, showing them basic operation of the nozzle on what they learned was a standard inch and a half hose. The rookies quickly learned the inch and half with a variable nozzle would be their primary tool in fighting structure fires. Both the pumper and the brush truck were equipped with a spool holding hardier rubber hose with a smaller variable nozzle. This would be their godsend for grass fires.

"This is more fun than a rodeo dance," Judy said as her team finished nozzle training. She worked side-by-side with Kathleen, Pookie, Joe Bob, and Curley.

"Speak for yourself," Curley said. He was soaked from the top of his bald head to his now squishy cowboy boats. He hadn't been ready for the power of water pressure when he took his turn at the nozzle. "Damn thing reared up on me like a crazy colt," Curley said after the Dulson firefighter helped him bring nozzle and hose back under control.

"Hell, Curley, laughing at you has been half the party," Joe Bob said.

Tiny Pookie surprised them all when she took a turn at the nozzle. When the pressure hit, she simply dropped to one knee, leaning into the nozzle and maintaining better control than most of the other rookies. Each trainee had a chance to run the nozzle, but they were taught to always work in pairs, with one firefighter leaning into the back of the nozzle operator to help with control, especially when water pressure was high to increase flow and reach. Judy was Pookie's backup, but she wasn't really needed.

Their team learned quickly during their turn at the Class A pumper, Ted showing them the process of initial pump engagement from the truck cab, switching the transmission from drive to the Power Take Off for the pump. They then worked at the panel just behind the driver's side door, learning how to prime, turn on tank to pump, adjust pump speed and pressure, and open valves according to which outlet water should be directed. Ted then gave a quick familiarization on emergency lights, sirens, and radios. Judy felt certain she couldn't retain it all at once, but it was a start. They would need more practice.

They were the last team to go to the brush truck. Guy saw them coming. He turned his back to the group, turned off the pump at the rear of the brush truck, wound in the hose using the powered recall, and jumped in the cab. Judy and her team stood stunned as their "chief" simply backed the truck into the station bay.

After parking the truck, Guy looked at their team.

"It's getting late." Almost under his breath, but still loud enough for them to hear, Guy mumbled, "And I've already trained the real firefighters."

Curley's bald head turned red, and he balled his hands into fists. Joe Bob placed a hand on his arm, stopping him as he started toward Guy.

"He's not worth it, Curley. We can learn better from Ted anyway."

"Dick head," Pookie said.

"There you go again. Hitting the nail square on the dick head," Judy said.

"Nasty little sucker, isn't he?" Kathleen commented.

Judy turned to Joe Bob. "I don't know if Pookie and Kathleen noticed earlier, but I think I learned something important when we first got here."

"He's scared shitless of women," Kathleen said.

"You saw?" Judy asked.

"I wanted to say 'boo' just to find out if he'd pee himself," Pookie added.

Joe Bob gave his mustache a nervous tug. "That information just might come in handy."

As Brad backed the pumper into the station, Guy called for everyone to go into the community building for some final business. Muddy, wet, and tired, the fledgling firefighters still chattered merrily as they moved inside and took seats around tables. Guy took a stack of papers and pens from the counter beside the kitchen and passed them to the group.

"I need everyone's clothing sizes, including shoe sizes. Answer all the boxes and blanks on these forms. I'll be ordering PPEs for everyone tomorrow," Guy said.

"PPEs?" Brad asked.

"Personal Protective Equipment," Pookie answered. Judy wasn't the only one reading her *Essentials of Firefighting*.

Guy glared at the tiny woman.

"It's bunker gear for structure fires and wildland gear for grassland…forestry too, but we don't have any of that around here," Guy said.

Ted Rome watched from the doorway. "No bids?" he asked.

"We'll be using a state approved vendor," Guy answered.

"But you don't have your state allocation to buy equipment," Ted said.

"It's been approved. This vendor knows me. He's willing to take and fill the order knowing they'll get paid as soon as we get our state money."

"You certainly move fast, Guy," Ted said.

"The faster we move, the sooner Coldwater will be safer from fire and accidents." Guy responded. His words seemed civil, but his eyes were cold and angry. He moved closer to Ted. "Thanks for your help tonight, Chief Rome, but I can handle training from now on."

Ted stood silent for a long time. His expression was cold and set. "The County entrusted me to train this company. I'll be back next week."

"Thank God," Kathleen whispered. Judy gave her lover's hand a quick squeeze. She felt the same way. Ted was an ally they desperately needed.

Chapter Fourteen

Metal and Fire

I feel like I'm having an affair," Kathleen said as she finished writing sizes and serial numbers on the equipment section of her fire department personnel file.

Brad blushed. "I'm not cheating on the Chief. He just doesn't understand ranch girls. He thinks you're a bunch of fluff bunnies who are afraid you might break a nail."

"Sometimes I'd like to pound a nail into his head," Pookie said.

"Pookie!" Kathleen hissed.

Judy sighed. "I should get after you too, Pook, but the truth is, I agree."

"Aw Judy," Brad responded. "He knows a lot about firefighting. We're lucky to have him."

"So what about us? Is he afraid Curley and I are going to break a nail?" Joe Bob asked.

Brad shuffled paper work on the desk. The station was complete, and Ted Rome had scrounged up surplus office furniture from storerooms at the City and County. For the most part, in just six weeks, the Coldwater Volunteer Fire Department was in business. Bob Hanks, the same absentee ranch owner who donated money to build the station, had contributed two computers, a Bluetooth enabled printer, and a year's satellite internet service.

"Aw, heck, Joe Bob. Damned if I can figure what Guy has against you; maybe he's afraid you'll try to take back chief. All I know is he's doing a bang up job training me and the boys," Brad said.

Judy snorted with humorless laughter. "I haven't seen you act like this since high school football. Remember that crazy coach you had junior year? Guy's got you all in matching t-shirts and strutting around like you're the 'jocks' of Coldwater."

"Well," Brad cleared his throat. "Maybe we are. I mean, a firefighter needs to be quick and strong, so being young and athletic isn't a bad thing."

The five clandestine firefighters stared at each other, exchanging expressions of amazement.

"Did he really just say what I heard him say?" Curley asked.

Judy collapsed into a chair, elbows on the desk and her head in her hands. "Sometimes, when you claim a soul brother, you have to remember it's for better or worse."

Joe Bob's face reddened. "Brad Kenton, you listen to me. There's more to succeeding at anything, firefighting included, than how fast and strong you are. He's got you young bucks horn-swaggled. Man hasn't called an officers' meeting since we elected him. That's not leadership, that's...that's...piracy. That's what it is, piracy. He's flat taken over our fire company, and maybe he should be worried about me taking back chief."

"Brad, I'm the duly elected treasurer, and he won't let me near any of the financial records. I'm really worried; all of us officers are responsible for the company, including the finances," Kathleen said.

"Well, the financial records are right here." Brad walked confidently to a file cabinet and pulled so hard the cabinet rocked when he tried to open a drawer. The drawer stayed firmly closed. "Oh, I guess Guy locked it."

"I know. I already tried," Kathleen said.

"And why didn't he call any of us to come get our gear?" Curley asked. "He called you and that gaggle of boys he's got following him."

"I'm sure it was just an oversight," Brad said. "Besides, I came down here to make sure you got your stuff as soon as Joe Bob called."

"Aren't you afraid your 'Chief' is going to catch you?" Judy asked.

"Naw, I'm just doing my job. Besides," Brad looked at his boots, visibly embarrassed. "Besides, he went to Albuquerque to meet with some fellow who sells fire engines. He won't be back until day after tomorrow."

"That's okay, Brad," Kathleen said, a note of resolution in her voice. "We're just glad you're issuing our equipment."

"After we're all done, I need to show you some basics about the radios and how to wear the gear. Guy showed us some neat tricks, like leaving your bunker pants stored over your boots so you just step into your boots and pull the pants up by the suspenders."

"Peachy keen," Pookie said, enthusiastically. It was time to play with the new toys.

⁂

The smell of acetylene and ozone filled the air. Wearing heavy gloves, Judy held a bent section of metal they'd cut from an old truck hood. Judy taught Pookie how to use each piece of equipment, including the welder, but Pookie was the artist. Pookie found the metal, cut, bent, and shaped each piece, and decided where it would go on the sculpture taking form on the metal workbench. Judy was just the assistant, having no real purpose in the process except to hold pieces or fetch tools. Pookie was a natural at welding, learning quickly. Judy held the metal tightly, a welding mask over her face, as Pookie ran the welder, protected by her own mask. When the bead was complete and the latest addition to the sculpture firmly attached, they both stepped back, expertly flicking their heads to pivot the masks from faces to the tops of their heads.

Pookie breathed deeply. "I really love that smell," she said.

"Don't tell Kathleen."

"Why not?"

"When she first came here, Brad and I didn't hear her drive up while we were repairing a seed drill. She watched us weld for several minutes and burnt the heck out of her eyes. She had to spend two days in a darkened room, putting ointment in her eyes every few hours."

"Oh wow! Is that why she decided to go to town today, because we'd be welding?" Pookie asked.

"I'm sure it had something to do with it, but, you know Kathleen is more of a girlie girl than either of us. Sometimes she just likes to get her hair and nails done and maybe shop for some clothes."

"At Walmart?" Pookie asked, astounded.

"Well, there's actually a couple of ladies' dress shops downtown, but you probably didn't notice."

"No way! Two dress shops, and I have to get my

art supplies at Walmart!"

"Sad but true," Judy said. She turned her attention to the rapidly forming metal sculpture before them. It was a test – about one eighth the size of the piece intended for the community center – but it was obviously a buffalo. It didn't have the polish and detail of most of Pookie's other work, whether one-dimensional or three. Instead, there was a different kind of appeal, made all the better by the fact that it was created entirely from scrap. "Pookie girl, I don't think you should finish the pieces in adobe and glaze. I think your metal sculpture is just fine."

"I'm done for today." Pookie walked around the piece, her head cocked to one side as she studied it. "I think you may be right. This is turning into more than just a frame for the finish."

"Looks damn good, if you ask me," Judy said.

Pookie smiled.

The two worked together storing welding equipment and putting away clamps and other tools. Judy flexed her shoulders, working out the kinks from the intensity of bending metal to their will.

"Kathleen said she'd pick up a pizza before she came home," Judy said.

"That sounds awesome."

The shop was silent after hours of listening to the sizzle and hum of the welder. Judy walked to the old refrigerator that they kept in the shop and pulled out two cans of Dr. Pepper, handing one to Pookie. She grabbed one of the makeshift chairs her father had built from old tractor seats and spare rebar and set it just inside the open shop door where a cool breeze came in from the outside. Pookie retrieved a chair for herself and took a seat near Judy. They sat drinking soda and staring out on the prairie, on land the Proctor family had stewarded for three generations.

"I never would have imagined I'd be living on a ranch, and I had no clue how much I'd love it," Pookie said.

"I thought you looked like a llama in a herd of cows when you first arrived," Judy said.

"Changed your mind?" Pookie asked.

Judy squinted one eye and studied her young companion, seeing the blue hair and studded dog collar Pookie wore almost all the time. "Well, you still look like a llama, but you're a darned good addition to the herd."

Relaxation ended abruptly when both their radios emitted a high-pitched tone.

"Shit," Pookie said.

"Damn," Judy added.

An electronic voice emitted from both radios.

"Dulson dispatch to Coldwater Fire. Dulson dispatch to Coldwater Fire. We have a grass fire near mile marker thirty-two on Highway 287. Structures threatened. Repeat, a grass fire near mile marker thirty-two on Highway 287. Structures threatened."

"That's the Johnson place," Judy said. Her hand shook as she pulled her radio from her belt and hit the talk key. "Coldwater four and fifteen responding," she said, using the language Brad had taught them all.

As they both jumped to their feet, rushing toward Judy's pickup, they heard over the radio. "Coldwater two responding." A pause. "Coldwater three responding." Pause. "Coldwater twenty responding."

"Good, that's Brad, Joe Bob, and Curley," Judy said, as she started the pickup and put it into gear. She started to spin gravel as she left the yard and mentally forced herself to calm down. She remembered Ted Rome's caution. At one of the first training session, he'd told the new company of firefighters that more firefighters are killed or injured going to a fire than they are fighting fire.

Judy felt a twinge of bitterness as she waited to hear more responders. There was no one from the gaggle of young men Guy was training. That wasn't a surprise. It was the middle of a workday and most of them had jobs in town.

"Coldwater two to Coldwater four," they heard over the radio.

"You take it, Pook. I want to concentrate on driving," Judy said.

Pookie picked up her radio. "This is Coldwater fifteen for Coldwater four. She's driving."

"Fifteen, you'll get to the station before us. Take the brush truck as soon as you get there. We'll follow with the pumper," Brad said, his voice clear but distorted over the radio waves.

Once they were clear of the workshop and could see in the distance, they both spotted the smoke. Judy guessed the fire was no more than three miles from the fire station. She drove with the emergency flashers blinking and as fast as she felt safe, not worrying the least about speed limit.

"Damn, that's right near the Johnson homestead," Judy said.

"Do I know them?" Pookie asked.

"Old couple in their eighties. They don't get out much. I've got about 500 acres of their grassland leased." She leaned forward, getting her bearings on the fire. "Oh Hell, that's our grass burning." She kept her attention on the road, but still glanced repeatedly at the smoke. "Only looks like an acre or so though."

"Hurry!" Pookie said.

"I am!" Judy responded.

Judy barely had the truck stopped and in park before they were both on the ground and pulling gear bags from the backseat.

"Wildland gear or bunker gear?" Pookie asked.

"It's a grass fire. I guess wildland," Judy answered.

They both pulled Nomex coveralls, helmets, and gloves from their gear bags. Since they were already wearing tough boots, they didn't change to the lace-up boots with the thick soles they'd been issued for wildland. They did throw into the brush truck both pairs of wildland boots, along with packs and the "jiffy pop" fire shelters required at all wildland fires. The shelters were a last-ditch effort for a firefighter to deploy if they knew they were about to be over-run by a fire. If Harold had had one, he probably wouldn't have been burned. Ted had said all those items were required gear but more for forest fires than prairie fires.

"Still, if you have to work for long putting out spot fires where the grass has burned, you'll be glad you have those boots," Ted had said.

Pookie hit the button to open the bay door as Judy started the engine. Judy paused on the concrete apron outside the bay, waiting as Pookie hit the button to close the door and then jumped into the passenger seat.

"You remember what Ted taught us about sirens, lights, and radio?" Judy asked.

Pookie answered by hitting the switches to turn on the siren and light-bar. Judy accelerated out of the yard and onto the state highway, heading toward the fire. Pookie picked up the microphone to the truck radio and hit the talk key. There was a loud squeal before they both remembered to turn down their hand radios to prevent reverberations. Pookie hit the key again and spoke into the mic.

"Coldwater Unit Two out of station," she said.

The disembodied voice of Dulson dispatch responded. "Copy that. Coldwater Unit Two out of station at fourteen, thirty-two hours." Ted had already told the Coldwater company that response records were kept based on a military twenty-four-hour clock.

Judy had no idea how slow a firetruck could seem as it raced to a fire. She remembered the face of Mrs. Johnson and her kindnesses over the years – soup when Judy's mother was recuperating from an appendectomy when Judy was just a girl. Eating oatmeal cookies and visiting in the Johnson living room when she'd gone with her father when they'd first formalized the land lease agreement. She drove and prayed, prayed for the safety of a wonderful old couple.

Since they'd leased the burning pasture for fifteen years, Judy knew exactly where to go. Pookie turned off the siren as they pulled off the highway and stopped at a wire gate.

"Leave the gate down," Judy called as Pookie jumped from the truck.

Just as they'd been taught, Judy drove to the rear of the fire. She recalled painfully the drastic mistake they'd all made the day Harold Kenton was so badly burned. The memory was especially acute when she spotted the elderly Thomas Johnson beating at the flames with a gunnysack. The fire was less than an eighth of a mile from his house.

"Coldwater Unit Two on scene," Pookie said into

the microphone as Judy pulled the truck to a stop just behind the fire.

"Dispatch copy. Coldwater Unit Two on scene at fourteen, forty."

They jumped out of the truck and ran to the rear so they could start the pump. The used brush truck was equipped with two person-sized cages, one on each side of the truck bed.

Judy turned on fuel to the pump and hit the starter button. It revved immediately and she breathed a sigh of relief.

"Pook, get in the cage on the left side, and be ready with the nozzle on the hose reel," Judy said.

Pookie was set in place, nozzle in hand by the time Judy had the water pressure set. Judy jumped in the cab and moved the truck to run alongside the fire. From the bed of the truck, Pookie sprayed a dispersed stream of water. They were both surprised at how quickly they were able to move along the leading line of the fire.

"Coldwater Unit One leaving the station," came over the radio, but Judy barely noticed as she concentrated in keeping the truck in the right place to support Pookie's fire suppression. When they reached the head of the fire, Judy stopped the truck, opened the door, and stood on the running board to call directions to Pookie.

"Get on the other side and hang on," she said.

With amazing agility, Pookie climbed over the top of one cage, and into the other, never dropping the nozzle from her hand.

Driving quickly through the black of already burned grass, Judy drove to the rear of the second flank of the fire, and they repeated the same procedure until the most threatening wall of flames was out. Just as they were finishing the second flank, the pumper truck pulled up beside them.

"Coldwater Unit One on scene," Judy heard Joe Bob's voice say over the radio.

"Dispatch copy. Unit 1 on scene at fourteen, fifty-three."

Brad stepped down from the driver's seat of the pumper and walked toward where Judy had stopped the brush truck. Joe Bob followed closely behind. Judy rolled down the window.

"Nice job, Judy girl," Brad said.

Joe Bob laughed happily, glancing between Judy and where Pookie still stood in the personnel cage on the truck. "You girls sure did it," he said.

Pookie smiled down at her fellow firefighters. "That was more fun than just about anything I've ever done," she said. She looked at the plastic window on the brush truck water tank. "But we're nearly out of water."

"Looks like you got it to me," Brad said.

Joe Bob looked at the blackened grass. "We still need to put out those hot spots. Good wind come up and those cow pies will start it all over again."

Brad held a hand up to Pookie, helping her jump down from the truck. "Come on, kiddo. The pumper has plenty of water. We'll run a hose over and fill you up."

Old Mr. Johnson walked toward the firefighters. He looked tired, and soot smudged.

"I heard y'all had started a fire company. Was sure darned glad to see you show up," he said. As he got closer, he leaned down, looking directly at Judy's face. "Why Judy Proctor, is that you?"

"Yes, it is, Mr. Johnson. How's the wife?"

"Good enough to hen peck me. She'll give it to me good tonight. I'd dumped the trash barrel down in an arroyo. Heck, it had been two days since I burned trash, but I guess there were still some embers."

"Looks like it," Joe Bob said.

Pookie approached the group, smiling at the old man as she climbed back on the truck and put the open end of a hose down into the refill outlet on top of the water tank. As soon as it was placed, she waved at Brad, who then opened the valve from the pumper to start water down the hose.

"And who's this young fella?" Mr. Johnson asked.

Judy laughed. "Mr. Johnson, meet Pookie Thompson. She's staying with Kathleen and me and helping out on the ranch."

"She? You mean a couple of girls saved my home?"

"Yes sir, it looks that way," Joe Bob said.

"Well, I'll be jiggered," Mr. Johnson said.

Pookie removed her helmet as she waited for the tank to fill, wiping sweat from her forehead. Mr. Johnson stared pointedly at her blue hair.

"Young lady, looks to me like you stepped into a paint can,"

Judy laughed. "Yeah, Pookie's kind of the peacock of Coldwater Volunteer Fire."

Joe Bob took a step back, speaking to both the women. "I just want to know one thing," he said.

"What?" Pookie asked.

"Did either of you break a nail?"

Guy Guyette's trip to Albuquerque exceeded all his expectations. He'd already submitted the Assistance to Firefighters FEMA grant application and felt certain the brand new company would be a cinch to obtain funding for its first custom built water tender, fully rated to serve also as Class A Pumper for structural firefighting. The addition of a third engine would enhance the state's rating of Coldwater Volunteer Fire Department to a full station rather than a substation, increasing state allocations by at least $50,000 per year. The meeting with his old buddy at Harold's Fire Supply and Equipment had gone well, very well indeed. They already had the truck specced out and could be ordered as soon as the grant was approved.

The sun was just setting as Guy opened the personnel door to the station, a bag containing a burger and fries in his hand. He'd check the office and eat his fast food dinner before he drove to the ramshackle farmhouse that was his temporary home. Guy's mood couldn't have been better when he sat at desk and hungrily attacked the burger. His mood was great, until he noticed the report, written in Brad Kenton's broad script, in the in-basket. As he chewed, he read. The burger was almost gone when he lost his appetite and threw the remainder of the burger back in bag.

"Bitches," he mumbled as he read of Judy and Pookie's successes at Coldwater Volunteer Fire Company's first official fire. His upper lip curled into an ugly sneer and then morphed into a nasty smile as an idea revived his good mood. Guy cranked up the computer and opened the NFIRS website. He was the only one with access since he guarded the password like sacred script. For the most part, the report he typed was accurate in every detail. Times, location, number of acres burned, cause of fire...they were all correct. Only the names were changed to attack the innocent. Guy's appetite returned as he inputted the names of the heroes in Unit Two. Responders: Coldwater One, Guy Guyette, and Coldwater Two, Brad Kenton.

"Fuck those bitches," he said. "Damned if they'll get the credit for our first fire call."

Chapter Fifteen

Test of Friendship

Judy punched the code into the combination door lock of the fire station, then she twisted the handle and pushed hard against the heavy metal door, so hard she hurt her shoulder when the door didn't budge.

"What the hell?" Judy said. She shivered in the light drizzle, the last remnants of a summer thunderstorm that had soaked the thirsty prairie earlier that day. She tried the code again, pushing more tentatively. The door stood closed and forbidding. *I know that's the right code,* Judy thought. She looked up at the grey sky and trotted back to her pickup. When she first arrived, she'd left her slicker on the back seat, expecting only brief exposure to the rain. She donned the slicker, feeling only slightly warmer and a tad clammy from the damp shirt underneath the waterproof slicker. Judy pulled her cell phone from her pocket, looking for Brad's number on the speed dial. She hadn't hit "send" when she noticed Brad's pickup on the highway, driving toward the station. Judy stepped inside her truck, waiting out of the rain until her unofficial brother arrived. Brad parked beside her and they both rolled down windows so they could talk.

"Why you out in the rain?" Brad asked. "It's not a training night."

"Guy hasn't returned my calls or email. I came down to leave a note."

"About what?"

"Remember my friend, April Sims, the reporter from the *Amber Globe-News*?"

"Sure do. She and Sophia helped look after the folks when Dad was in the hospital," Brad responded.

"She wants to do an article about what it's like to start a new fire company, especially out here in the boondocks."

Brad's face lit up with his contagious smile. "That would be awesome."

"I suggested she come over next Tuesday when we do training, but I wanted to make sure all the officers knew about it."

Brad's smile faded slightly. "I'll have to check with Guy, but I don't see why not."

Judy's irritation increased. "Brad, you'd think Guy was king of the world, the way you talk about him."

"Well, he is the chief."

"Yeah, he is." Judy sighed and decided to change the subject. "Hey, something's wrong with the door lock. I couldn't open the station."

"Oh, Guy changed the combination yesterday."

"Why?"

"He says if we change it every month or so, the station will be more secure."

Judy laughed. "Brad Kenton, we don't even lock our houses out here. Why do we need to change the station locks so often? What if we'd had a fire? I couldn't have gotten in to the trucks."

Brad climbed out of his pickup and walked toward the office door. Judy followed. The drizzle had dissipated. They air was heavy with moisture, a wonderful thing on the semi-arid plains.

"He emailed the combination to me and the boys. We could have gotten inside."

Judy was still damp and clammy with the predictably accompanying mood. Irritation exploded into anger.

"You and the boys? What about the rest of us?"

Brad cleared his throat and changed his posture, standing tall, like a man of authority. "Judy, you just got to get over it. Guy has picked the fastest and the strongest. If you're going to be a firefighter, you gotta pull your weight."

He turned his back to Judy, a movement that communicated dismissal.

Judy moved like a cougar, swift and decisive. The concrete apron was clean and shiny from the rain, but the dirt to the side was still soft from recent construction, offering a nice bed of mud. She tackled him from the side, leaving him off balance, then she grabbed his right ankle, flipping him into a sizeable mud puddle.

"What the hell!" Brad yelled, trying to stand, but slipping and sitting back down hard in the slimy mud. "What's gotten into you?"

"Brad Kenton, we've worked side-by-side since we were kids. When have you ever known me not to pull my weight?" Judy stood at the edge of the concrete apron, fists clenched at her side.

Brad managed to lumber to an unsteady standing position in the slippery puddle. He gathered into an attack position, his right fist cocked for a punch.

"Come on," Judy hissed. "I whipped you when we were kids, and I can whip you now."

Brad paused. Slowly, his body relaxed, and his contagious smile looked starkly white against the mud on his face. "Damn it, Judy. I bet you could."

"I could sure as hell whip Guy Guyette's ass."

Brad put his hands on his hips and studied his oldest friend long and hard. "You know what, you could." He cocked his head to one side, thinking. "Judy, he's not exactly the strongest and the fastest, is he?"

"He's the sorriest, if you ask me," Judy said.

Brad wiped at his muddy face with his hand, succeeding only in smearing more mud on himself. "The code's two-two-five-three," he said. "Would you open up for me? I think I'm going to need to use the shower in the men's room."

Judy's anger swirled away, evaporating into some other universe. She fought to contain a fit of the giggles.

"Don't clog the drain," she told him. She hit the buttons for the combination and opened the door. "Want me to bring in your gear bag? You could wear your wildland gear home."

"I better. If I walk in the house like this, Julie's likely to tear into me too, and I don't think I could take being whipped by two women in one day."

"What you two do in the bedroom is none of my business," Judy teased.

Brad raised one eyebrow as he entered the station. "Wouldn't have dawned on me. Could be you just told me more than I want to know about you and Kathleen."

They were friends again. Judy felt a relief from a tension she hadn't even fully realized was there. Brad was her brother, her partner in crime, and he always had been. For a while, she hadn't been sure he was still there to watch her back.

❧ ❧ ❧ ❧

"Who the hell are you?" Guy Guyette asked.

April Sims didn't budge. Instead, she raised her camera and took another shot of two young firefighters as they demonstrated how to don a Self-Contained Breathing Apparatus (SCBA).

"Didn't you hear me?" Guy said, a little louder.

April turned and smiled at the red-faced man. "I'm April Sims from the *Amber Globe-News*."

"The media can't be here without the chief's permission," Guy said.

"All the other officers approved her coming," Brad said from just behind his company chief.

Guy turned abruptly. He stared at his young deputy chief with a facial expression that could best be described as gob-smacked.

"What's got into you, Kenton?" he demanded. "Haven't gone soft on me, have you?"

A silence had descended. All activity stopped, and a cadre of six young men, part of Guy's handpicked lackeys, gathered close, listening intently.

"You need to listen to the Chief," said Billy Marsh, grandson to Halbert Marsh. He was just months out of boot camp, starting his four-year enlistment in the Texas National Guard.

Guy gave a sly smile, nodding encouragement at his chosen few. He smiled until Brad turned on the young man.

"Listen, yes, but that doesn't mean we stop thinking." Brad glanced toward Judy where she'd moved to be close to April after she saw the confrontation between reporter and chief. "Just 'cause some fella comes in with all kinds of certificates, that doesn't mean that our first loyalty shouldn't be to our friends, our families, our community."

Guy stood noticeably taller as he turned to face Brad. "This is insubordination, son. I expect you to step down as deputy chief."

Joe Bob stepped close to Guy. "Not likely." With unplanned choreography, the occupants of the station changed position, circling the old cowboy, expressing a respect for his authority that had nothing to do with his title. "He was duly elected by this company, and he'll stay deputy chief as long as this company says he's deputy chief."

Guy's face went from red to pale. He took two steps back, and beads of sweat appeared on his forehead. "Well...well...the chief has to be in charge. At a fire—"

"Yep, at a fire, it's important for the Incident Commander to be in charge, but I been talking with Ted Rome. The company elects the officers and the officers are responsible for company business."

Guy turned to April. "Who invited you here?"

"I did," Judy said.

"We did," Kathleen corrected.

"She's a good friend and a fine reporter," Judy added.

Guy focused his full attention on Judy. He gave her a look that touched a cold core of fear somewhere in Judy's heart, but she stood firm, her gaze never wavering.

"Well, you folks have fun out here. I'll be in the office doing some real fire business, none of this publicity stunt stuff." Guy turned abruptly and strode into the office, slamming the door behind him.

There was dead silence throughout the station. Joe Bob looked at his fellow firefighters. "I think all you folks got things to do, don't you?" he said.

The group scattered, returning to the tasks begun before the confrontation.

"If you'll excuse us for a minute, ma'am," Joe Bob said to April, "We need to do a little company business, and I sure hope this hasn't put our company in a bad light for your newspaper."

April smiled. "I'm here tonight for a human interest story about one rural fire department, reflecting on how important you volunteers are to everyone in the Panhandle." She looked toward the closed office door. "But I wonder if, in time, there's not another important story here." April pulled her notepad from a vest pocket and walked toward the two young men who had gone back to SCBA training. The officers of Coldwater Volunteer Fire watched as she moved away, and Joe Bob motioned for them to gather close.

"Is that true what you said, Brad, about the officers being in charge of company business?"

Brad smiled sheepishly. "It will be if we ever get our act together and pass bylaws."

"Don't worry, Joe Bob. Martha and I got sample bylaws from Ted Rome, and we're working on a draft now," Kathleen said.

"Joe Bob, you know the company elected you chief…maybe that's the way it should still be," Judy said.

The old ranch foreman rubbed at his stubbly chin. "We need to ease into this. Guy's got us hog-tied until we can get the financial and company records out of his hands. Let's get these bylaws done for now…take our time and do it right."

Chapter Sixteen

Meanwhile, Back in Amber

Pookie was surprised how different it was to drive a pickup in city traffic. A native of Colorado Springs, she was no rookie to city driving, but a half-ton truck wasn't like her mother's low-slung sedan. She'd grown comfortable maneuvering the old rattletrap feed truck or even Judy's newer Ford pickup around the rutted roads of the ranch. She'd had no misgivings about driving when Judy offered to loan her the truck for a trip to Amber. Judy and Kathleen sent her with a short list of items to pick up from the health food store and an over-sized ranch supply store, things not to be had in Dulson. She had the list, but they didn't fool Pookie. Her benefactors were giving her a chance to spend time with Terry, a chance to visit her new girlfriend on Terry's own turf.

After asking Pookie to make the shopping trip to Amber, Judy had focused on pouring another cup of coffee.

"You know, it's an awful long day driving to and from Amber and doing all the shopping," Judy said.

Kathleen turned her face to hide a sly smile as she picked up her empty breakfast plate and walked toward the sink. "And motel rooms are kind of expensive," she said as she placed the plate in a sink of soapy water.

Judy cleared her throat. "If you wanted to stay

the night…well…maybe you could stay with a friend."

Pookie didn't bother to answer before rushing up the stairs to her room. She'd hit the speed dial on her phone for Terry's number while still on the stairs.

"Damn it," Pookie said the second time she jumped a curb while turning a corner. There were no curbs on the ranch.

She had completed her city errands and drove out of the business district of Amber toward the quieter neighborhoods near the university where Terry worked and went to school. The electronic voice of the GPS on her cell phone led her confidently to the address for Terry's apartment. Pookie half expected the bossy voice of her electronic guide to comment on the curb induced bumpy journey, but no such criticism ensued.

"You have reached your destination on the right," the business-like voice said, and a street view picture of the tiny duplex appeared on the phone screen as Pookie parked the truck in front of the real thing. Pookie sat for several minutes, waiting for her pulse rate to slow. She hadn't seen Terry since they'd become intimate, emotionally and spiritually as well as physically. Weeks had passed since Terry visited the ranch with April and Sophia. The pair made full use of the unlimited minutes on their cell phones during the interim, but the thought of seeing, touching, smelling, and tasting Terry once again made Pookie lightheaded.

Finally, Pookie opened the door and climbed from the cab to the street, starting for the front door. She was half-way through the tiny front yard when the front door swung open and Terry rushed outside. It was a cross between a collision and an embrace when they came together. Pookie had been afraid there would be an awkwardness at first, but she felt instantly at home in the circle of Terry's arms. The kiss they exchanged was more like hunger than passion. Pookie finally pushed slightly away, glancing around the neighborhood.

"What will your neighbors think?" she asked.

Terry laughed. "Most of them will think the woman I've been telling them all about is finally here." She tilted her head to one side, thinking. "Except Mrs. Burrell. She'll think the whole younger generation is damned to hell and will probably put us on the prayer list at the First Pentecostal Church."

"Nice to know she cares," Pookie responded.

"Nosey and mean, that's what she is," Terry responded. She leaned down to pick up the small duffle Pookie had dropped on the sidewalk, leaving both arms free to greet her lover. "Speaking of Mrs. Nosey, let's get inside. I can't wait to show you my place."

Terry paused momentarily, looking toward a tiny 1940s vintage Cape Code style cottage across the street. She smiled, waved, kissed her right hand, and then, with great exaggeration, blew a kiss toward the cottage.

"Mrs. Burrell's house?" Pookie asked.

"One and the same," Terry answered.

They walked together toward Terry's front door. "Does she really watch that closely?" Pookie asked.

"It's really rather pitiful. She sits in a recliner, looking out that window all day, every day. If she's not watching, it's because she's in the bathroom or making a quick meal in the kitchen."

"What about Mr. Burrell?"

"Rev. Burrell," Terry corrected. "He died several years ago."

"Poor woman," Pookie said.

Terry opened the screen door, motioning Pookie

to go inside, but she dropped the duffle and put her hand on Pookie's arm, stopping her just before she entered the small duplex apartment. She gazed intently into Pookie's eyes.

"That's one of the things I love about you," Terry said. "You care, even about people who hate you."

Pookie smiled. "Learned that from my dad. If people hate me because I'm different, that's their problem, not mine."

As they stepped into Terry's austere living room, Pookie stopped. She rotated in a slow circle, taking in every aspect of the room. The furniture was a mixture of Goodwill second-hand and Walmart particleboard cheapies, all rather typical college "digs." There was a floral pattern loveseat with decorative placemats over the arms, not entirely successful in hiding the worn material beneath, and an office-style black recliner with a footstool. Pookie recognized it as a frequent Office Max sale item. Four cinder blocks with a plank across the top served as a coffee table, and a small desk rested against the wall; its obvious age and chipped paint did nothing to detract from its utilitarian nature – along with the cheap secretary's chair beside it. Books and papers cluttered the surface with a laptop computer placed as the focal point on the desktop. A printer was on the floor beside the desk. College texts, with a few novels lightening the intellectual weight, filled a particleboard bookcase. Pookie was pleased to see both Tony and Anne Hillerman mysteries among them as well as Anne McCaffrey sci-fi. Pookie loved those fictional worlds and felt yet another bond between her and her lover. The shelves were full and a stack of overflow rested beside the bookcase. A tiny television sat atop the case, and Pookie could see attached to that television one of the antennas that picked up High Definition television without requiring paid cable or satellite.

Pookie savored the feel as well as the facts of the room. With an obviously limited budget, Terry managed to imbue a warmth and personality to the space. A poster of Vincent Van Gough's Starry Night was taped to the wall above the loveseat, and a decorative candle rested in the center of the makeshift coffee table. A homemade banner saying, "To thine own self be true," hung above the desk with a bumper sticker below it saying, "Well-behaved women rarely make history."

Terry stood, obviously breathless. "Why…why do I feel like you're seeing me totally naked?"

Pookie took Terry's hand and faced her lover. "Do you mind me seeing where you live?"

"Mind? No. Terrified? Yes," Terry responded.

Pookie stepped close, wrapping the taller woman in her arms. She stood on tiptoe, placing her mouth near Terry's ear.

"Don't fear me, love," she whispered. "I adore what I see, whether it's your soul or your body."

Terry wept. She wrapped Pookie in an embrace so tight, Pookie had a little trouble breathing. Terry put her head on Pookie's shoulder, and sobs bubbled up. Wounds old, deep, and buried found release. Terry wept as only someone who has experience deep pain can do once they have found a truly safe haven. Pookie held Terry tightly, reacting not in the least as the shoulder of her Gov't Mule t-shirt became increasingly damp and just a little bit snotty. When it became apparent this would be far more than a brief cry, Pookie pushed gently away, took Terry's hand, and led her to the loveseat, where they both sat. Terry took her place once again with her head on Pookie's shoulder, their arms held tightly around each other. In time, the sobs eased, replaced by sniffles and a pronounced case of hiccups.

Finally, Terry backed away and grasped the tissue box from the coffee table. She took three tissues from the box in rapid succession and used all three as she blew her nose.

"My, aren't I attractive?" Terry said. She turned her red and swollen-eyed gaze toward Pookie.

"You are to me," Pookie responded.

"Even now?"

Pookie reached up and pushed a strand of tearfully damp auburn hair from Terry's face. "Especially now," she said.

Terry looked at Pookie's shoulder and gasped. "Oh my God, your shirt," she said.

Pookie contorted face and neck so she could see the object of Terry's distress. "Yeah, looks a little like I was attacked by a jelly fish."

"I'm so, so sorry."

"Why?" Pookie sighed and shook her head, searching for words. "You honored me with your pain. That's well worth a sloppy shirt."

Terry pulled a new tissue from the box and wiped ineffectually at the damp shoulder. "Did you bring extras?"

"Yeah." Pookie glanced toward where her duffle still rested in the middle of the living room. "Ummm… maybe it's time you showed me your bedroom."

Despite still swollen eyes, Terry's face brightened. "I had planned on showing you the campus first."

Pookie laughed. "I meant so I could change

shirts."

Terry gestured widely with both hands. "There are three doors. Bet you can guess which is the bedroom."

Pookie looked to see the front door, the back door exiting from the tiny kitchen and one interior door. "Bathroom?" Pookie asked.

"Off the bedroom," Terry answered.

A drying tear still glistened on Terry's cheek. Pookie wiped it away with her thumb. "Come with me. You can wash your face before we go see the campus."

"I must be a fright. Do I have raccoon eyes from the mascara?" Terry said.

"Yep."

"Oh God."

"It's kinda cute."

"So you say."

Terry gently pulled at a sleeve of Pookie's shirt. "Does this material dry quickly?"

"Yes."

"Give it to me. I'll wash it in the sink."

Pookie nodded agreement. "Cool! Then I'll have a clean shirt in the morning, but first … ahhhh, I really need to pee."

"You can do that while I wash the shirt." Terry blushed. "That is if you don't mind me being in the bathroom while you…"

Pookie laughed. "And so, we achieve a whole new level of intimacy."

Chapter Seventeen

Trial by Fire

Dreams shattered like plate glass on concrete. It was the first time for all three at the Proctor Ranch to experience that sensation – the heart stopping immediate jump from sound sleep to adrenaline rush.

The fire radio Judy and Kathleen left on each night in their bedroom and its counterpart upstairs in Pookie's room violated the night with a page tone that did just what it was supposed to do. No way in the world would anyone sleep through that electronic scream. Judy jumped straight out of bed and stood barefoot on the cold, wood floor, standing in a fighting stance, facing the radio. Kathleen sat bolt upright in bed, a dazed look on her face.

It was 2:04 a.m.

"To all Coldwater firefighters." The dispatcher's voice blared over the radio. "We have a structure fire at mile-marker thirty-two on Highway 385. Repeat, structure fire at mile-marker thirty-two on Highway 385. All available personnel respond."

Pookie didn't knock as she swung the bedroom door open and stood just inside the door, still struggling to slip on shoes and wearing a t-shirt backwards.

"What do we do?" Pookie said.

Judy calmed herself, remembering Ted Rome's

voice as he told them what to expect.

"Pee first," Judy said. "Then we go."

The radio came to life again.

"Coldwater One responding," Guy's voice said.

"Coldwater Two responding," said Brad.

"Coldwater Three responding," said Joe Bob.

Judy had the radio in her hand. "Coldwater Four, Seven, and Fifteen responding," she said.

Others followed, but Judy stopped listening. It was enough to know Coldwater Volunteer Fire Department was turning out in force. Judy knew from Ted's training that a busy dispatcher was maintaining a communications log, one that would be critical for the after-action reports.

Before Judy finished, Kathleen was already out of the bathroom and jumping into jeans. "Your turn," she said to Judy. Pookie had disappeared, Judy assumed into the half-bath off the back porch. Ted said it was important to take those few minutes to pee because that avoided one major complication at the fire scene. Judy grabbed the clothes and boots she'd worn the day before and rushed to the bathroom.

All three women were dressed and out the door in less than five minutes. Judy and Pookie's gear bags were already on the backseat of Judy's supercab truck; Kathleen paused briefly to grab her bag from the trunk of her car, and Judy helped her throw it into the bed of the truck. All three jumped in the cab, and Judy spun gravel as she shoved the truck into gear, snapping her seatbelt as she drove. Kathleen reached over to the dashboard and hit the button for the emergency flashers.

"Mile marker thirty-two...that's the Haskell place," Judy said.

"Jesus, I hope they're okay," Kathleen said.

"Isn't Mrs. Haskell the one who makes the awesome carrot cake?" Pookie asked.

"That's her," Kathleen answered.

As Judy sped down the county dirt road, the truck did a brief fishtail. Kathleen placed a hand on Judy's forearm. "Slow down, honey."

Judy took a deep breath and slowed slightly. The truck felt immediately steadier on the dirt road.

A voice came over the radio and there was an annoying echo with all three radios going at once. Since Judy needed her hands to drive, Kathleen and Pookie turned down the volume on their hand-held units.

"Dulson One and Fourteen responding in Dulson Engine Ten," Ted Rome said.

"Dulson Five and Twelve responding in Dulson Engine Two," a strange voice said.

All three women sighed audibly. "Thank God Ted will be there," Kathleen said.

"And Engine Ten is their water tender. Remember the drop tank training we did," Judy said. They left the county road and Judy barely paused as she pulled onto the highway, just a mile from the Coldwater fire station. They were the closest and would likely be the first at the station.

"Ted can shuttle water from the station. We don't have to worry about the pumper running out of water. What's Engine Two?" Pookie said.

Judy tried to remember from her visits to the Dulson main fire station. "I think that's their old Class A pumper. I'm sure they'll keep the main pumper in town in case it's needed there."

The pickup swung into the fire station lot, and Judy parked close but out of the path of the truck bays. All three women jumped out while the pickup was still rocking slightly, grabbing gear bags as they went. Pookie hit the combination on the personnel door, throwing it wide open as Judy helped Kathleen retrieve her gear bag from the truck bed. Once inside the station, they unzipped their red gear bags and each woman stepped into bunker boots and pulled bunker pants—ones with legs already tucked over the boots— up by the suspenders. They had each practiced the process a hundred times and the training paid off. They were fully geared up, including coats and helmets, in under a minute. Pookie hit the button to open the bay door for the pumper and Kathleen hit the button for the door in front of the brush truck.

"You and Pookie take the pumper," Kathleen yelled. "I'll bring the brush truck."

"Good plan," Judy responded. As she climbed into the driver's seat of the pumper, she paused to turn on the main switch that connected the truck's two batteries. She started the truck and pulled it onto the concrete apron. Pookie hit the red button to close the door and ducked outside as soon as the truck was clear. She jumped into the passenger seat, buckled her seatbelt, and started lights and sirens as Judy drove the truck onto the highway. Pookie picked up the microphone to the truck radio.

"Engine One leaving Coldwater station with Coldwater Four and Fifteen on board," she said.

"Dispatch copies. Engine One out of station at oh two, fifteen hours," dispatch responded.

Brad's voice was next on the air. "All other Coldwater personnel report directly to the fire scene," he said.

"Coldwater Three copies," Joe Bob acknowledged.

"Coldwater Engine Two leaving station with Coldwater Seven on board," Kathleen said over the radio.

"Dispatch copies. Engine Two out of station at oh two, sixteen."

Judy looked toward the Haskell Ranch headquarters, not four miles from the fire station. She dared to feel hope when she failed to see the yellow and red flicker of flames in the distance. Unbidden, a joke she's overheard Guy Guyette tell his cadre of young, male converts came to mind.

"What's the motto of a rural fire department?" Guy had asked.

"What?" a dutiful firefighter responded.

"Haven't lost a basement yet." Guy rarely laughed, but he laughed at his own joke, and Judy wasn't sure if it was her own prejudice or a real observation, but she'd felt an anxious twitch as she listened, her ears detecting a hint of evil in that laugh.

Whether she liked Guy or not, there was a kernel of truth to his humor. Distance and lack of fire main water systems made it particularly difficult for a rural fire department to actually save a structure. The thought made Judy press the accelerator just a little harder, and she consciously made herself ease up, maintaining an awareness of the maximum speed she could achieve while still feeling a confidence of control in the massive vehicle she drove.

"We're going to save this house," Judy mumbled.

"What?" Pookie half-yelled, striving to be heard over the siren.

"Nothing," Judy said. She paused to think. "When we get there, you start setting up the hoses and pump. I'll turn off the propane and electric."

"You got it, boss," Pookie responded.

They turned off the highway and down the half-mile of dirt road to the Haskell homestead. There was still no sign of flames. Judy really began to hope. As they pulled into the yard, Judy finally saw the flicker of red and yellow she'd dreaded. It was visible through the windows of the barn and workshop.

"Thank God. It's the barn!" Pookie said.

Judy heard Ted Rome's voice in her head, like a new and highly active conscience.

"Always allow for engine egress at a fire," that voice said.

She assessed the layout of the farm yard and backed the truck into an empty spot about ten yards from the barn. She pointed the nose of the truck toward the driveway, so that it could be easily driven away should the fire spread or the situation become suddenly hazardous to firefighters and their equipment. A small tendril of smoke escaped from an unseen gap between wall and roof in the barn. That hint of smoke gave Judy one more critical piece of information – wind direction. She picked a spot upwind from the fire, remembering the many hazardous chemicals almost every farmer or rancher stored in the barn. Pookie shut off the siren but left the emergency lights flashing as Judy parked the truck.

"Coldwater Engine One on scene," Pookie said into the truck's radio mic.

Kathleen's voice followed immediately over the radio. "Coldwater Engine Two on scene."

"Copy, Coldwater Engines One and Two on scene at oh-two, twenty," the distant dispatcher responded.

Kathleen stopped the brush truck in the driveway near the pumper. She leaned out the open window of the truck.

"There's not much water in this truck." Kathleen looked around, obviously assessing the situation. "I'll park over by the house in case we need to cool the propane tank or use it for flare ups by the house."

"Good idea," Judy responded. "Then it will be out of the way when the city's tender and pumper get here."

While Pookie pulled hose to fully extend the pre-connect one line from the truck, Judy broke into a run, hampered by her heavy bunker gear, toward the propane tank. Ben Haskell stopped her when she'd only gone a few feet.

"I already turned off the propane," he said.

"What about electricity?" Judy asked.

"The breaker box is inside the barn," he responded.

"We'll have to pull the meter," Judy said.

"Show me how." They both half-ran toward the main utility pole on the property. Ben yelled breathlessly, "When this is over, I'm joining your fire department," he said.

"You'll be welcome," Judy responded. "Where are Delia and the kids?"

"In the house. Should I send them away?"

"No, they're probably safer there for now."

"We would have slept through it, but the dogs woke me barking," Ben said. "I smelled the smoke as soon as I stepped outside."

"Where are the dogs?"

"In the house."

When they got to the pole, Judy used the spike end of the fire axe she'd taken from a rack on the truck to break the wire on the contraption the electric company used to show that there had been no tampering with the meter. Ted's voice in her head continued to walk her through every step. She firmly grasped the glass meter, pulling it from the power box. Once the contacts were free and the flow of electricity stopped, she replaced the glass meter in a sideways position.

"Why'd you do that?" Ben asked.

"If we spray water this direction, the sideways meter keeps water away from the live connections." Judy picked up her radio and keyed the mic. "Coldwater Four reporting that both propane and electricity are secured."

Guy's voice responded. "Coldwater One copies. Propane and electricity secured."

As she spoke, she heard a vehicle pull into the yard. She sighed with relief as she saw Brad's truck as he backed it into a spot well away from the action. A second sigh of relief followed as both Brad and Joe Bob jumped from the truck and rushed toward the pumper, each man already dressed in full bunker gear.

"What can I do now?" Ben asked.

"Truthfully, wait in the house with your family. We'll let you know if we need anything. If you have a way to make coffee without electricity or propane, we'll be wanting it soon," Judy said.

When Judy arrived at the pumper, Brad and Joe Bob already had SCBAs pulled from the compartments where they were stored. Brad had one air tank and regulator system on his back, and was snugging the mask into place. Joe Bob was just donning tank and harness. Pookie already had both pre-connect hose systems pulled and the lines charged with water. Judy grabbed an SCBA, Ted's voice once again walking her through the process of securing the harness, placing the mask and Nomex hood, and adjusting her helmet to fit over the entire contraption. As she prepared for interior attack, Brad looked carefully through the window of the barn, assessing the situation. Two more vehicles pulled into the yard. Judy recognized Guy Guyette's vehicle in the lead. The personal vehicles backed in beside Brad's truck, and Guy walked at an almost leisurely pace toward the pumper, his white helmet reflecting moonlight and proclaiming his authority as chief. Three of the younger firefighters walked behind him.

"What's the situation?" Guy asked Brad. Guy picked up the last of the four SCBA units and began to gear up.

"Looks like it's contained against one interior wall for now, but there's a lot of black smoke," Brad said.

"Situation is ripe for a backdraft as soon as we open a door or break a window," Guy said.

Much to her surprise, Judy was relieved to see to Guy, to have access to his experience.

"What now, Chief?" she asked, her voice echoing through the open mouthpiece of her air mask. She could still be heard clearly. Although she'd turned on the airflow from the tank, none of them had placed the regulator in their masks. They were conserving air for fighting the fire.

Guy looked at Judy. Surprise flashed across his facial expression. "I'm the only one here who has actually fought a structure fire." He turned to Judy. "You and I will be Attack Team One. We're going inside."

Judy's heart felt like it stopped and then restarted at a rapid pace.

Guy turned to Joe Bob. "You'll be Incident Commander for now." He turned his attention to Brad. "Get one of the boys here geared up to work with you as Attack Team Two. You be ready to relieve Judy and me when we come out."

"Maybe one of the boys and I should—" Brad said.

"You've got your instructions. Do it!" Guy turned to the three young men waiting for directions. "The other two of you, you man pre-connect two. I'm going to break a window. We'll let it go ahead and backdraft if it's going to before we open that door. You'll be doing exterior attack through that window. Got it? Start after I break the window. Give it a minute or two to see if the windows blow out, but start cooling it off before we go in."

"Yes sir," one young man responded with the other two nodding agreement.

Judy picked up the nozzle from one of the two charged lines. She glanced back and saw Pookie working at the control panel on the side of the truck. Judy felt the push of pressure on the hose as Pookie adjusted the pump, increasing the pressure so that they could effectively attack the fire. An intense wave of pride in her young friend momentarily replaced the heart pounding fear Judy felt at her pending entry into a burning building for the very first time. She turned her attention back to the job at hand, as she carried the nozzle and dragged the hose so that she was in place to enter the personnel door into the barn. Now fully pressured, the hose was awkward to move, almost like fighting a muscled creature into place. Brad moved further down the hose, dragging a length into place to make her job easier. Judy knelt, holding the nozzle at the ready and inserted the fitting for the air regulator into her mask. She gave a hard exhale, activating the regulator. The coolness of the compressed air felt wonderful and the comfort of the air and the sound of her breath, enhanced by the Darth Vader sound of the regulator, helped to ease her fear. She had trained well and trusted her equipment.

The second hose team was in place, ready to hit the interior from an exterior window as soon as Guy broke the glass. The Chief had taken a six-foot pike pole from a rack on the side of the pumper and stood to one side, the barn wall to his back as he used the pole to break the glass. For a few moments, black smoke billowed from the window opening, and then, as Guy had predicted, a bright yellow and red shone from inside and a rush of air broke out the rest of the windowpanes. Judy had just witnessed her first backdraft. Guy motioned frantically for the second hose team to move forward, and the two young men positioned the nozzle in the open window and opened the water spray to a coarse mist. Immediately, the bright colors of the fire inside lessened from the cooling effects of the water. Guy walked to the personnel door, pulling back the backside of his left glove as he did so. He used the bare back of his hand to test the temperature of the door, then turned toward Judy, using a "thumbs up" signal to ask if she was ready. She returned the gesture and the game was on. Guy inserted his own regulator into his mask, pushed the door open, and then rushed to his position as number two nozzelman immediately behind Judy. Together, they moved inside the barn, Judy adjusting the nozzle to a coarse mist, straight enough to be directed toward the flames and fine enough to offer an umbrella of protection for her and her teammate as they moved into the burning structure.

It was an odd juxtaposition for Judy's brain, a sensation she didn't know if she would ever be able to explain. Her thoughts and senses went on triple speed and at the same time slowing to what felt like a near stop. She saw everything in slow motion as she entered the building. All fear was gone, in its place a cold intelligence so profoundly intertwined with animal instinct that it was impossible to know where one stopped and the other began. She had never felt more alive. Ted's voice remained in her head, taking on a life of its own like an alter ego. The training she'd undergone walked her through every step as she spotted the primary source of the flames and used a subtle clockwise rotation of the water flow, directing it at the base of the fire. She directed the nozzle toward the back of the flames, noting that the flow of water from the exterior attack team was already having a beneficial effect. She directed the stream from the nozzle she held to work in collaboration with their efforts. She felt Guy's shoulder against her back. He held the hose in the crook of his arm and worked with her to move the heavy hose, aiding her as she directed the water flow. In a momentary flash, Judy felt an intense camaraderie for the man at her back. She knew in that instant that no matter what the differences out in the world, a bond formed between those who face fire together.

Then it was gone – the supporting shoulder, the aid in positioning hose and nozzle. She had no idea why, but Judy realized, beyond a doubt, that she alone now faced the flames before her. She continued to work, focused even more intently on lessening the fire. Then the whole world shifted and her life changed.

Homemade shelves, heavy and awkward, rested

against the wall beside where Judy worked. She'd barely noticed their presence, briefly thinking about the potential hazard from any toxic or flammable materials that may be stored there. She'd even taken a moment to direct water from the flames to soak she shelves, hopefully decreasing the likelihood that material there would ignite and create a second fire front.

Those shelves became her primary focus. She jerked her gaze away from the fire as her peripheral vision caught a flash of motion behind her and to her left. She looked just in time to see those shelves as they shifted and tilted, a giant presence falling directly on top of her. Judy jumped, still holding the nozzle tightly. The jump was only partially successful. Her upper torso cleared, but her legs were pinned beneath the heavy shelves. She felt sharp pain in her left leg and hip, each pain tied to where the hard surface of a shelf connected with her body. She heard the varied sounds of tools and cans and seed sacks from the shelves as they hit the floor. One sound in particular filled her heart with cold fear – the sound of a can hitting the concrete and then rolling, a liquid gurgle as its contents escaped. An intense flash followed as the flammable contents reached the open flames and only her bunker gear and the water mist prevented Judy from severe flash burns.

"Left for life," Ted's voice said in her head, somehow making its way past the most intense panic she had ever known. Judy instinctively reached for the control valve on the end of the nozzle, turning it harshly to the left, as far as it would go. The nozzle now surrounded her in a halo of fine mist, a water bubble protecting her from the flames, but not entirely from the heat of the steam as water met fire.

Panic, pure panic. The intelligence and animal

instinct had deserted her, and Judy struggled uselessly against heavy shelves, unable to pull herself free. She screamed inside her air mask, with no one to hear but herself.

"Remember the film," Ted's voice said, and with a clarity so intense, it was as if Judy was back at the station, sitting in training. The film had been about wildland fire shelters and how to survive if a firefighter deploys the "jiffy-pop" shelters of reflective material just large enough to provide a thin layer of protection for a single firefighter. The biggest threat was panic, the irrational desire to throw the shelter aside and run. The man being interviewed had burn scars on hands and face and was missing part of one hand.

"I remembered my family. They needed me to come home, so I stayed in the shelter, and I lived," the man said.

Judy envisioned Kathleen's face. In seconds, she saw the peaceful features of her sleeping lover… Kathleen riding across the pasture…cooking enchiladas …sharing the over-sized recliner with Judy as they watched a movie on television.

Judy's panic eased. *I choose to live*, she thought

The intensity of the original flames had increased ten-fold, but the flames lessened in her immediate vicinity as it consumed the immediate influx of flammable liquid. Judy adjusted the flow of the water to more of a stream and tried to reach the flames, but the fallen shelving was in the way, splashing more water back at her than hitting the fire. Judy paused to think, assessing her situation. She changed the nozzle to a straight stream and directed it toward the ceiling until she achieved a perfect ricochet, and water hit the flames directly. The fire began to lessen immediately.

"Your PASS device," Ted's voice screamed in her head.

Judy leaned against the hose beneath her so that she could hold the nozzle with one hand. She reached to the harness that held her SCBA in place and found the small box that was her Personal Alert Safety System and punched the button on the side. The screeching alarm that had so annoyed her when they checked the batteries in the station sounded like an angelic chorus to her now. It was doing its job, screaming that there was a firefighter down. Almost immediately, she felt the weight of the shelving eased against her leg. Through the dark, she saw the vague shape of two firefighters working beside her, lifting the shelfing off of her. From movements alone, she recognized her soul brother, Brad. It took the strength of both men to lift the heavy shelves. As soon as they reached the tipping point so that they leaned against the wall once again, Brad grabbed the strap at the nape of her neck on her bunker jacket and began dragging Judy toward the door. The other firefighter—Joe Bob—took the nozzle from her hands as they passed and turned his attention to the fire.

Judy tried to struggle to her feet, relieved to realize that neither leg nor hip appeared broken, but Brad dragged her so quickly that she only flailed helplessly. Only when they were past the barn and several yards into the yard did he stop, and Judy was able to pull herself to an upright position, standing unsteadily. She removed the regulator from her mask, punching the button that stopped the airflow as she did so.

"You okay?" Brad's muffled voice yelled through his still operational air mask.

"I'm bruised and shaky but okay. Go back in and

help Joe Bob," Judy said.

"Where's Guy?" Brad yelled.

"Hell if I know. He just disappeared right before the shelves fell," Judy answered.

"Hope he's not still in there," Brad yelled then ran back into the barn.

Judy felt a strong arm go around her waist, supporting her. She looked up to see Sally Lyne, the EMT from the Dulson Fire Department, beside her. Ted Rome and Pookie stood close as well, desperate concern on their faces.

"You need to sit down and let me assess you," Sally said.

"Sounds good to me." Judy licked parched lips. "I could really use a bottle of water." One appeared in her hand, and she wasn't even sure who handed it to her. Judy limped as Sally led her away from the barn and toward the brush truck where Coldwater Fire Department kept the EMS equipment. "Where's Kathleen?"

"I sent her back to your station in the water tender with one of my firefighters so she could show him where to refill with water," Ted answered.

Judy felt intense relief that her lover had not been there to witness how close she'd come to disaster.

"You okay, Aunt Judy?" Pookie asked. There were tears in the girl's eyes.

Judy patted Pookie on the cheek. "Little bruised and maybe scorched a tad, but I'll be fine. Go take care of your truck, Miss Engineer," Judy said.

Pookie turned and ran back to the truck. Judy glanced to see that Pookie had already arranged placement of the folding drop tank to hold water from the tender and had started putting a suction line in place to refill the pumper from the water the tender had dumped in the tank.

"That little girl is hell on wheels," Ted observed.

"No shit," Judy responded.

Ted scowled toward her. "Brad said Guy went in with you. Where is he?"

"Hell if I know. He just disappeared," Judy said.

"When that shelf fell?"

"No, before."

"I'm right here," Guy said from behind Ted. They both turned to face him, seeing clearly that he stood unscathed, barely any soot on his new bunker gear.

"Where were you? I could have been killed," Judy said.

Guy more smirked than smiled. "There's always more of a risk for inexperienced rookies."

"I'm not a rookie," Ted said. "From where I stand, Judy did just fine. I want to know why you, an experienced firefighter, deserted your team member during an interior attack."

A glint of hate flashed across Guy's face. "I'm the chief here, and I'm not accountable to you."

"The Hell you're not! The Commissioners designated me as County Fire Marshall. All the departments are accountable to me," Ted said.

Guy paused, his mouth open. "When did this happen?"

"Commission meeting last month." Ted's eyes narrowed and he glared at Guy. "Seems they were a little concerned how some of the local chiefs were handling things."

Something caught Guy's attention and he looked toward the pumper. Ted and Judy followed his gaze and watched as Pookie directed two of the young firefighters in setting up a two-and-a-half-inch line with a gated "Y" so that they could divide that into two more one-and-a-half-inch attack lines.

"What's that girl think she's doing telling my boys what to do?" Guy demanded.

"She's following the instructions of the Incident Commander," Ted said.

"I *am* the Incident Commander," Guy said.

"The Hell you are," Ted responded. "You turned it over to Joe Bob, and he assigned it to me as soon as I got here."

"Well, I'm taking it back!"

"No, you're not. Damned if I'll turn IC over to an experienced firefighter who abandons his partner in a burning structure," Ted said.

"I...I just went to assess the situation."

"What were you assessing when I was pinned under those shelves?" Judy demanded.

Guy's initial answer was a silent stare of hate. "I found another door; we can do interior attack from that side as well."

"You should have done that as IC before you went in on an attack team," Ted said.

Guy hawked and spat, the wad of spittle landing between Ted's boots. "Well then, I guess you don't need me here, do you?"

"Neither need nor want," Ted answered.

Guy turned to walk toward his truck.

"Leave the SCBA," Ted called.

Guy didn't stop walking as he released the buckle on the belt, shrugged out of the harness, and dropped the whole rig on the ground, obviously not caring if he damaged the unit.

"Bastard," Ted mumbled.

"Chief, I want to go back in," Judy said.

"Not until I check you over," Sally said.

Ted laughed. "You heard her. Even the Incident Commander has to do what the EMS folks say."

Judy was bruised and would be limping for a few days, but she was lucky. In many ways, the look on Kathleen's face when she heard of Judy's close call hurt Judy more than the bruises. Still, she would fight fire again that night, even going back into the smoldering interior. After all, her daddy taught her to always get back on the horse.

Chapter Eighteen

About Guy

Guy Guyette stank of smoke. He didn't notice the smell as he hung his bunker coat on the peg by the back door. He pulled wide, red suspenders from his shoulders so he could drop his bunker pants, still tucked around bunker boots. He stepped free of the boots and pushed the ensemble of boots and pants against the wall below the coat, all ready for him to step into at the next fire call. Last but not least, he hung his helmet on the peg over the coat. Guy paused briefly, taking time to notice the acrid and distinctive smell of house fire still emanating from his bunker gear. He breathed deeply, feeling comfort in the familiar scent. Being a firefighter was his world, all he had known for thirty years, ever since he became a junior firefighter through the Boy Scouts Explorer program at the age of sixteen, a beneficiary of a local program for disadvantaged teens. It saved him…almost. At least it had for twenty-five years. Then…then his department opened to women.

Fucking bitches, Guy thought as he slipped on the loafers he kept by the back door and headed for the kitchen in the dilapidated farmhouse that was his temporary home. He ran water into the sink, waiting a few minutes for the tinge of red from rusty pipes to clear. Then he filled a teakettle and placed it on the stove. It was an old habit. No matter how late the fire call nor what time of day or night he finally made it back to the station, Guy always made a cup of instant coffee. Oddly, it relaxed him more than anything else he'd found, giving the crisis induced adrenaline time to dissipate from his system so he could sleep.

As he waited for the water to boil, the itching on his back became unbearable. He stripped off his t-shirt, exposing a back covered in scars, over fifty little puckered circles. One in particular pained him the most, no matter how many years passed. It had been the first, and in so many ways, the most painful. He backed up to an exterior wall corner and scratched mightily, trying to ease the itch of fifty scars, including the one that was his greatest torment, one on his upper back, near his right shoulder. As happened so often, for an instant, the itch and pain of that one scar took him back, made him a time traveler, making him a five-year-old once again. It was the first burn…the first of many.

❧❧❧❧

The boy sat on the back steps like he did so often…alone. He longed to play with the kids he could hear yelling in a happy cacophony during their sandlot ball game in the empty lot near the rental house that had been his home for over a year, the longest he and his parents had been in one place. He wanted friends, the company of other children, but his mother forbade it.

"Stay away from them kids," she'd demanded. "None of their nosey folks' business what happens in this house. I see you playing with any of that lot, and I'll hide you within an inch of your life."

That was one of the dark times, the ones he

dreaded the most, the moments when it was so hard to remember that his mother could smile and laugh. He preferred the light times, those moments when she might even treat him to a batch of the refrigerator cookies she bought on sale at the Piggly Wiggly. Those times were almost always when his daddy was home, a break between making a living on one of the off shore oil rigs in the Gulf. His father was a mysterious presence in his life. Although his father was a silent and taciturn man, Guy never doubted his father's love, but he never understood how to reach him, this mysterious presence so often absent from his life. The most affection he remembered from his father was an occasional pat on the head and a soft expression on the man's face as he watched his son play. Guy couldn't know for sure, but he always suspected that a smile was hidden below his father's ample mustache, a smile to match the twinkle in his eyes.

Guy wanted to know his father, but during those times when he was home—between the big jobs on oil rigs—Guy's mother was so possessive of his father's time and attention. Even as a toddler, Guy felt moments with this man, almost a stranger, were stolen seconds while his mother napped or went to the store. Guy missed also the meager attention from his mother. His father's presence seemed to exacerbate the relatively benign neglect that substituted for maternal love. It worsened when they moved from the small town where his parents had grown up to Houston. At five, Guy vaguely remembered the added care provided by grandparents, even his mother's high school friends. Now, he was alone, but then, so was his mother. Once, she had spent hours on the phone with friends or reading different fashion and women's magazines while Guy played on the floor of the living room, enjoying the toys his father always brought when he returned from the oil fields.

In the city, the magazines and phone calls lessened, then disappeared. In their place, a bottle of clear liquid now resided permanently on the end table beside the couch, an overly full ashtray as its companion. Guy's new job was to constantly monitor the state of ice in his mother's glass, gently taking it away to replace melted ice with fresh from the automatic dispenser on the refrigerator. Once, curious at his mother's fascination with the clear liquid from the elegant bottle, Guy had snuck a sip, choking on the fiery contents.

"Now don't you spill my drink," his mother called as she heard him cough.

"I won't, Mother," Guy responded, rushing to get ice, hoping she wouldn't discern his transgression in drinking the forbidden liquid. He would never repeat this mistake.

Guy still enjoyed the toys, his secret world of imagination on the living-room carpet, surrounded by plastic people and animals, cowboys and Indians, spacemen, farmers, policemen, soldiers. He especially loved the tube of exotic animals his father bought on the best day of his life, the day the three of them had gone to the zoo.

Sometimes Guy would interrupt his play and stare at the strange woman sitting in his father's recliner. He wondered where his beautiful mother had gone and how this disheveled individual in a pink housecoat, with stringy, dirty hair had taken her place. He lived for those moments when he could glimpse his old mother, hear her laughter, and enjoy those seconds when she focused her full attention on her only child.

As Guy sat on the back steps that day, he

remembered that mother, and he longed for her. His father was gone again and had been for a long time. The last parting had been different. Guy had hidden in his room, frightened by the angry words he heard between his parents. Finally, after days of tension, his father mysteriously appeared in the middle of the night, sitting on the edge of his bed. Guy blinked sleepily, confused at this unexpected intrusion. His father was silent for a long time.

"Do you…do you know I love you, little man?" his father asked.

It was the first time Guy had heard those three magic words from his father. It would be the last.

"Yes," Guy lisped through sleep-deadened lips.

It wasn't his customary pat on the head. Guy's father gathered the boy into his arms and held him close for a very, very long time. For the rest of his life, as he drifted to sleep, Guy would remember that moment, perhaps his most precious.

Then his father was gone. Guy would be fourteen before he learned of his father's death a few months after that sad farewell, the victim of one of the all-too-frequent fatal accidents of work at sea on the offshore platforms. Then it made sense to Guy, the life insurance and Social Security payments that sustained his mother's indolent lifestyle.

That day, that fateful day when Guy sat on the back steps, he wanted magic. He wanted his old mother and his missing father. He wanted to play with other children. He just wanted. It had seemed like a miracle when he spotted the purple flowers growing along the fence, an unexpected gift from a prior tenant who had planted bulbs. Guy jumped to his feet. Excited, he gathered two of the purple crocus and carried them hastily to where his mother sat in her chair, some soap opera playing on the television.

"Look, Mother, look. We have flowers," the boy said, holding his treasured flowers toward his mother, offering a gift of magic.

She turned bloodshot eyes toward the boy. "Don't you bother me during my shows! What do I have to do to get your attention?"

She grasped his shoulder painfully with one hand, a lit cigarette smoldering in the other. Maybe it was an accident that first time. Maybe it wasn't. Guy never knew. As she reached for his other shoulder with the hand holding the cigarette, the glowing tip dipped, burning through his thin shirt and into the flesh below. Guy screamed and fell to the floor. He looked, stunned at his mother, stunned at the hate he saw in her eyes.

"That'll teach you. That'll get your attention," she said.

At the age of five, Guy lost his belief in magic, vanished with the crocus crushed under his mother's pink slippers. As the boy looked at his mother, a word came to mind. One he couldn't remember how or where he learned it.

Bitch, he thought. The love for her evaporated that day, and he never again fully regained the skill needed to love, to feel tenderness.

And so it began, years of discipline via cigarette burn. In time, it would be his salvation from the hell that life with his mother would become. A third grade teacher saw him flinch as she gently touched his back when she leaned over his desk, checking his work. A trip to the nurse's office revealed his painful secret, the old scars and the fresh burns. Foster care proved cold and indifferent, but it was better...better than the increasingly incoherent and cruel mother and the mysteriously absent father.

❧ ❧ ❧ ❧

As Guy finished his long back scratch, he opened his eyes and his thoughts returned to the present.

"Women always fuck things up," he mumbled to himself, remembering how he had been fired from his job as a captain in a company where he'd worked for nine years, all because of his hazing of the newly integrated women firefighters. *They never should have been there,* he thought.

The kettle whistled and he shut off the gas burner, retrieving from the cupboard an old coffee cup, one with a Maltese Cross emblazoned on the side along with the name of his very first fire station. He spooned instant coffee into the cup, making it strong, finally adding the water to the dark mixture. The coffee did little to ease his mind. The bitches won tonight, and he knew it. He wanted to pack his meager belongs and go, but he needed to hang on a few more weeks, just a few more weeks. He sipped his coffee as he walked to the living room, and pulled three darts from a wooden board, a dartboard of his own making. Photocopies of three faces were stapled side-by-side on the board, ones taken from Coldwater Volunteer Fire Department personnel files. Kathleen Romero's face was on one side and Pookie Thompson's on the other. It was impossible to recognize the face in the middle it was so riddled with the holes inflicted by hundreds of accurately thrown darts.

"Bitch," Guy hissed as he threw a dart, placing it in the center of a ragged remnant of a photocopy of Judy Proctor's right eye.

Chapter Nineteen

Out-of-Town

Judy stretched, languid and naked across the unfamiliar bed, a towel spread beneath her to protect the decorative cover. The occasional cry of "ouch" when Kathleen hit a particularly tender spot accented her moans of pleasure. Kathleen's gentle touch spread tincture of arnica followed by oil infused with St. John's Wart on the bruises along Judy's left thigh and hip. It was very apparent where each shelf from the heavy storage case had slammed into her body. Judy's heavy bunker gear had helped but could not fully protect her from the falling fixture. Kathleen paused in her healing administrations to kiss Judy softly on the biggest bruise, the one on her hip. It was so deep that the center was yellow instead of blue or black. Kathleen sat up abruptly, making soft spitting noises and retrieving a tissue from the night stand to wipe at her lips.

"Yuck," she said. "St. John's Wart smells a lot better than it tastes."

Judy laughed and rolled onto her side, facing her lover. "No one said nursing me would be easy."

Kathleen kicked off her house slippers and stretched full-length beside Judy on the bed, wrapping her arms comfortably around Judy.

"No one said it would be easy loving you.

Especially when you insist on trying to get yourself killed," Kathleen said.

"I was *trying* to put out a fire. The nearly getting killed part was an unexpected bonus," Judy said

"Bonus! More like bone-headed." Kathleen raised up, leaning on one elbow. "I know it's useless to ask you to give up firefighting, but you damn well better promise to be more careful."

Judy pulled Kathleen to her, kissing her with a deep tenderness. Kathleen moaned, her body moving against Judy, the intensity of arousal only increased by familiarity with her partner's taste and smell and touch.

"Can I tell you a secret?" Judy whispered against Kathleen's cheek.

Kathleen laughed softly and pulled slightly away, just far enough so that she could look into Judy's eyes as she brushed a strand of hair from Judy's forehead. "What? You have kept a secret from me?"

"Not for long," Judy said softly. "You know, I almost panicked when that shelf fell and that can of paint thinner went off."

Kathleen gave a ragged breath and buried her face in the nape of Judy's neck. "Thank God you didn't."

"You know what saved me?"

"No."

"You."

Kathleen leaned away again, confusion on her face. "What?"

"I thought of you. I knew I had to do whatever it took to come home to you. I remembered your face. I thought of the pain it would cause you if I died. My mind went cold and clear because I couldn't bear the thought of leaving you," Judy said.

Tears filled Kathleen's eyes. One trickled down her cheek, and Judy kissed it away.

The two women had made love many times, in many ways, and in many places. Sometimes… sometimes, it was an experience that transcended the sexual. That night would be such a time. As mouths and hands explored, teased, and pleasured, there was an added resonance. Perhaps…perhaps it was when the joining of bodies reflected something unseen but intense. Their souls touched, humming in unison, enjoying the orgasmic pleasure of the spirit in a way that few people ever achieve. It was a night that neither woman would ever forget.

❧❧❧❧

The sound was muffled, but they heard it. Sophia laid the Sapphire Books novel she was reading across her chest, and looked over the top of her reading glasses at April, who lie snuggled beside her. Sophie knew April was still awake when a giggle caused April's shoulders to shake.

"Sounds like our guests are having a good time," Sophia said.

April sat up, the giggle turning into a quiet laugh. "Honey, if you'd come as close to kicking off as Judy did, I'd damn sure make certain you had a good time."

Sophie laid her book and glasses on the nightstand. "I'm so glad they accepted our invitation. A weekend away from all that mess is what they need."

April sighed and her lips tightened into a thin line. She moved her pillows so that she could lean against the headboard and then put her arm around Sophie. Sophie moved to a comfortable position they both knew, one they frequently enjoyed as they discussed their days before drifting to sleep. Sophie laid her head on April's shoulder, April's arm around her, and Sophia's hand resting on her lover's stomach.

"Sweetheart, we both know the world isn't fair, but it really sucks when it happens to your friends," April said.

"You at the newspaper, me as an attorney, yeah, we know life isn't fair. It's so wonderful when we go to the ranch…Judy and Kathleen…*Dios mio*…the purity of their life on the land…it gives me hope."

April rubbed at her chin with her free hand. "Sophia, Judy and Kathleen have plenty of courage. Out on the ranch they know how to do things where I would be clueless, but I don't think either one of them knows how to deal with a real scoundrel."

Sophia laughed the deep, sexy laugh that still made April's heart skip a beat. "Monday, *Querida*… Monday we'll start looking into the past of this Guy Guyette."

"If it looks like a rat, if it walks like a rat, if it smells like a rat, it's probably a rat," April said.

"I thought that was a duck," Sophia said.

"I'm a writer. I can take literary license."

This time, they didn't hear a moan from the guest room. It was a muffled scream.

"Well, I'm certainly glad we put a good, solid bed frame in the guest room," April said.

Sophia sat up abruptly, crossing her arms across her chest. "Hey! What do you mean you'd strive to please me if I nearly died?"

"Well, I would."

"I don't intend to cheat death if I can help it," Sophia said.

April laughed. "The best part about sticking my

foot in my mouth is what I have to do to make it up to you."

April leaned into Sophia's neck and nibbled, right in the spot she knew was so very, very sensitive. Sophia took a deep breath and closed her eyes, fully enjoying the sensation. Her right hand cupped April's breast, and her fingers teased at the nipple until April mirrored Sophia's sighs of pleasure. In a very short time, the two women neither heard nor noticed any further noises from the down the hall.

❧❧❧❧

Terry's usually neat bedroom was in shambles. A trail of two sets of clothing started in the living room, outside the bedroom door, and continued as a Hansel and Gretel trail all the way to the bed. One of Pookie's lace-up boots rested half-in, half-out the bookshelf by the desk and the second had been kicked away with such force, it would likely take some time for her to find where it now hid under the bed. Shirts, skirt, jeans, and underwear were scattered across floor, nightstand, and bed like the after-effect of a clothing bomb. The bed itself was equally as disrupted with sheets rumpled and covers askew. The two girls—young women actually— slept peacefully, oblivious to the mayhem surrounding them and both still as naked as the day they were born. That wasn't totally true. Pookie still wore one eyebrow ring.

They had planned to go out the prior evening, to enjoy the short-term mobility and freedom allowed with the use of Kathleen's car, loaned to Pookie for her visit with Terry while her benefactors enjoyed a weekend at April and Sophia's. Those plans evaporated as soon as they were alone in Terry's cozy duplex. A few easy kisses while sitting on the couch ignited a flame so intense, it surprised them both. What followed was a night of lovemaking more athletic than tender, but neither woman seemed to mind. They enjoyed the passion of youth, consumed by an intensity born as much of novelty and exploration as physical desire.

Pookie woke first. Her internal clock had grown accustomed to the early rising of life on the ranch. She lay for a long time, enjoying the feel of Terry's warm breath against her bare breast as Terry slept, using Pookie's tiny torso as a pillow. In time, other urges overcame the tenderness as she stared at this woman she'd grown to love so intensely. Pookie eased herself from under Terry, causing only a slight moan from the sleeping woman. Pookie padded on bare feet toward the tiny bathroom, where she enjoyed a long and pleasurable pee. Without thinking, she left the door open, not even conscious of the level of comfort she felt with her lover.

"Hurry up," Terry mumbled from the bed. "The sound of you peeing is making me need to go."

Pookie laughed as she flushed the toilet and washed her hands. "It's all yours," she said as she returned to the bed and crawled under the covers, slightly chilled from her naked journey to the bathroom.

Terry did close the door. Pookie smiled, oddly pleased at Terry's continued shyness. When Terry returned to the bed, she too eagerly sought the warmth of the bed, and of the woman beside her.

"Wow! What a night!" Terry said.

"I'll say," Pookie responded. She stretched languidly, but stopped abruptly, mid-stretch. "Ouch!" she said.

"What's wrong?"

"I think I pulled a muscle in my back."

Terry looked at Pookie, a concerned expression on her face. "Are you all right?"

Pookie laughed softly. "All right? I'm tee-totally awesome."

Terry leaned on one elbow, looking at Pookie. "So, what do you want to do today?"

"It's your home turf. What do you recommend?"

Terry's eyes sparkled with excitement. "Let's tour the campus, and I want to introduce you to some people."

"Sounds good. I'd like to meet your friends."

"Well...them too...but..."

"Yes?" Pookie encouraged.

"I thought you might want to meet some of the professors in the art department. I know it's Saturday, but there's a show opening in the gallery at the museum. They should be there."

"Art department? I thought you were in history and anthropology."

"I am?"

A confused wrinkle appeared between Pookie's eyes. "You're friends with professors in the art department?"

"No, silly, but I thought you..."

An awkward pause followed. Pookie felt a sudden twitch of unease somewhere in her solar plexus.

"You thought I what?" Pookie asked.

Terry sat against the headboard and pulled the covers over her chest. "I thought...well...Pookie, you're too smart not to want to go to college. And...and I graduate soon, but I know I can find work on campus, you know, if you were in school here."

For an instant, Pookie envisioned a flash of her

stepfather's face.

"I've already made all the arrangements." She heard his voice echo in her memory. "You're registered at the community college. Time to do something practical and productive," he said.

Pookie felt a twinge of the same tightness in her chest she'd known as her world turned upside down, when her stepfather tried to push her into a box of his making.

"I like where I am, what I'm doing now," Pookie said.

"But you have such a talent, such a mind," Terry insisted, leaning toward Pookie, as though her intensity could make her new lover see the light.

"Maybe. I'm using both right now. An artist couldn't ask for a better place to create than the ranch, and I'm learning more than I ever learned in any school, about ranching, about firefighting."

"Pookie, it's just not practical. There's no life for you there," Terry said.

Somewhere inside Pookie, there was a big red button, one she hadn't realized was there until Terry punched it. Even tempered as she normally was, the wave of anger, the feeling of being cornered and trapped, rose like bile in the throat of her soul.

"I think it's up to me to decide where and how I want to live my life," Pookie said, her eyes flashing with anger. She slid out of bed, and started gather the trail of clothing, donning individual items if she happened to locate them in the proper order.

"Pookie, please," Terry said, her voice quavering as she fought off tears. "I didn't mean to offend you."

Pookie sat on the edge of the bed, lacing the one boot she'd been able to find. She turned to face Terry, her face flushed with anger. "I walked away from my home, my mother—" Her eyes glistened with tears. "Because I wouldn't let my stepfather run my life. What makes you think I'll let you take over where he left off?"

"Pookie, I…"

Pookie stood abruptly and stomped lopsidedly around the room. "Where's my other fucking boot?"

"You…you kicked it under the bed," Terry said, crying.

Pookie knelt by the bed and then bent to look beneath. She snagged the boot, carrying it without pulling it on her socked foot. She grabbed the duffle she had yet to unpack and headed for the front door.

"Pookie!" Terry called, the anguish in her voice penetrating Pookie's wall of anger.

Pookie turned to face Terry, who now stood in the middle of her bedroom, the bedcover wrapped around her naked body.

"Terry, I…I lo— I really care about you, but I need some space. I need to think."

Terry nodded in mute agreement. Tears streamed down her cheeks. She opened her mouth to speak, but no sound came. She reached one hand toward Pookie's retreating back. She continued to stand there as Pookie left the duplex, closing the door behind her.

Pookie didn't know where she was going when she started Kathleen's car. Without making a conscious decision, she drove through the university neighborhood and headed west on the state highway that led to the Canyon State Park, a place she'd visited with Terry. She drove, fumingly angry, at one point reminding herself to ease up on the gas when she realized she was driving eighty mph on the two-lane highway. She didn't go into the park, instead pulling into a scenic overlook on the rim of the canyon, a geological wonder that appeared miraculously as one approached it over the flat prairie. From her vantage point, Pookie could look down miles of canyon, and see far below the river that had taken millenniums to cut this huge gash in the unbroken prairie. Pookie parked and walked to the overlook, a rail fence protecting viewers from the impressive drop at the canyon rim. She felt her anger settle and lessen as she watched a pair of red-tailed hawks swooping within the canyon. She enjoyed the rare experience of being able to watch a hawk from a position above the flying bird. They were magnificent.

As the anger simmered and calmed, another emotion bubbled to the surface. Unbidden, sobs clawed their way up Pookie's chest, catching briefly in her throat, and then finding voice in a wail, a sound she'd only made one other time in her life. Only her father's death had ever created this depth of grief and pain.

Pookie was confused. Yeah, the fight with Terry hurt, but like this...surely a little fight didn't merit this level of grief. Then, in her mind, she saw a face... her mother. It was that moment when her stepfather threw her out of the house for refusing to go to the community college, his choice for her. Her mother had watched, sad-eyed and silent. She'd let her daughter go.

"Why, Mom? Why?"

Don't ever lie to yourself, Pookie thought. The thought sounded very much like her father's voice.

Pookie thought about her mother. Frankly, when Pookie was growing up, the innocuous woman hadn't been much of a person to her. Her mother had always seemed remarkably able to be happy, whatever the circumstance. Pookie had lived for her father's attention and approval, but she'd never worried about her mother. Her mother was just there, always meeting their needs, whether it was a clean house and clothes or a hot meal. Pookie just assumed she'd always be there for her.

"Why, Mom? Why?" Pookie asked the massive canyon before her. "Why did you let him do it?"

Pookie realized she hadn't heard Terry's voice as Terry laid out her plans for Pookie's life. She'd heard her stepfather, planning and running her life, striving to humiliate and lessen her.

Terry had triggered the anger and grief. Pookie hadn't even realized how angry she was at her stepfather. She had no clue as to how much she grieved the loss of her mother.

Judy and Kathleen won't do that, Pookie thought. *I have mothers I can count on.*

Now that she reached the root of her emotions, Pookie recalled the conversation with Terry.

"Do I want to go to college now?" Pookie asked herself. "I don't know...maybe."

Pookie pulled her cell phone from her pocket. Terry picked up on the first ring.

"Pookie, come back," Terry wailed.

"Okay," Pookie said. "But on one condition."

"What?"

"Don't tell me what to do with my life?"

Pookie heard Terry give a shaky sigh. "Just so... just so, at least for now, you still want to spend at least a part of it with me."

Pookie wiped drying tears from her cheeks with her bare hand. "Yeah, Terry. That sounds good to me."

Chapter Twenty

Old Times

The dust was thick in the air as they pushed the last of the cows and calves through the narrow gate and into the corrals. In the dry summer air, the milling cattle stirred and raised the dirt like a wrecking ball dropped in a talcum powder factory. Without exception, the cadre of riders now wore bandanas over noses and mouths, looking more as if they were preparing for a stagecoach robbery than sorting calves from cows. The calves called a cacophony of complaint at having been removed from the life of freedom that had been all they had ever known. The process was nothing new to the mama cows, but they complained loudly anyway.

Harold Kenton rode like the cowboy he'd always been. True, he was on the gentlest of the Kenton horses, and he'd quietly rode drag with Pookie rather than taking point or flank with the more experienced and hardy riders. He was still healing, but, beneath the bandana, he wore a grin that said clearly that he was happy to be back in the saddle.

When they first started the day's work, Judy had watched Pookie as often as she could spare the attention. As boss and ramrod of the entire operation, she had to be aware of everything and everyone. She soon relaxed, realizing that in the herding of cattle,

Pookie learned as quickly as she had any other task set before her. Besides, Harold was at her side, and it had been Harold, along with Judy's father, who had taught her all there was to know about the cattle business. During the early process of gathering cattle, Kathleen had been there too, riding the new paint gelding they'd bought from the Strong Ranch in the Oklahoma Panhandle. Once the herd was gathered from the far corners of each pasture, Kathleen rode ahead, arriving at the house to help Martha and Julie Kenton prepare a meal for the crew.

Once the last of the cattle were in the pens and the gate closed, the cowhands dismounted, loosened saddle cinches, and gave horses the opportunity for a long cool drink from the stock tank. Horses were then tied in various shady spots for the long wait as the cowhands turned to the hard work of sorting cows from calves using the complex of alley, pens, and gates in the Handle P Ranch corral complex. Judy was responsible for assigning tasks, but there was no need. This team of friends and neighbors worked together often. Cowhands moved easily to positions staffing gates and pens. Only Pookie needed instruction, and they all had to adjust to Harold Kenton's light duty assignments. Normally, he would be Judy's second in command, watching the whole operation and ready to step into the breach if anything started to go wrong. Eye contact and a nod from Judy was all that was needed for Joe Bob to know he now filled that role.

Judy paused to study Harold's face. His grin was visible with the bandana removed from his face. Once the cattle were contained, the dust had settled somewhat, and they were all able to breathe easier without the cloth masks. Still, Judy noticed he was paler than he'd been when they started the day, and there was a strain to the smile. He was getting tired.

"Harold, can you show Pookie the ropes pushing small bunches into the alley so we can sort them? This is her first time. She needs a good teacher," Judy said. It was the easiest of the jobs, but she knew Harold would enjoy teaching the promising young cowhand.

"Sure thing," Harold answered. He walked to his pickup, reaching in the bed to retrieve two horse whips. He and Pookie would use them to encourage the cattle through the gate. The crack of a sharply snapped whip was usually enough to turn cattle when they headed in an undesired direction.

"Watch him. If he looks like he's getting over tired, let me know," Judy whispered to Pookie.

"Right, boss," Pookie said.

Judy raised one eyebrow and looked at her young friend. "Boss?"

"Don't worry. It's a compliment," Pookie said.

"So what do you think of your first cattle drive?" Judy asked.

"It's awesome." A pained expression flickered across her face. "My dad would have loved it."

Judy gave Pookie's arm a gentle squeeze before going back to work.

The two Bar-D cowboys strode into corrals and worked on foot to divide the crowded herd between the two large pens on the north side of the corrals, closing the gate between the two. Three slightly smaller pens were on the south side with an alley about fifteen feet wide in between. It was a simple system, really. Groups of ten to sixteen cows and calves would be pushed into one end of the alley, Judy would approach the bunch, whip in hand, with a person stationed at the gate at each of the three smaller pens. Judy would gently approach the bunch, working until she divided one animal from the rest. When that animal bolted past, Judy would call "in" if it went in the first pen and "bye" if it went to one of the other two. She would point with one finger of her right hand if it went in the second pen and two fingers if it went in the far pen. The hands operating the gates would open the gate where the animal belonged, closing it after them. It was pretty much a bovine computer practicing the very simplest example of binary thought. With cows and calves, it was even easier. For the most part, cows were "in" and calves were "bye" into the second pen. It would be a mix into the third pen. Any animal, cow or calf, that looked sick or in need of attention, was sent to that far pen.

It only took a couple of hours to sort the cattle into their respective pens. When that was finished, the cowhands remounted their horses and pushed the complaining cows out of the corrals, through the horse pasture and three miles across the pasture nearest the house to one out of ear-shot of the crying calves wanting their mothers. Weaning was never an easy process, whether mother and child was four-legged or two. The cows were difficult to herd, wanting to return to their babies, but they calmed some when they could no longer hear the calves. Once the gate to the far pasture was closed, the cowhands rode in loose ranks, talking and teasing as they rode, eventually urging their horses into a trot then a gallop, all eager to end the day's work. When they neared the house, they pulled back to a walk, none wishing to make their horses "barn-sour" – too eager to end a ride and therefore hard to control on the trip home.

"It's just like old times," Brad said as he pulled his horse in step with Judy's.

"Old times, new times, future times…heck, Brad, you and I were born to raise cattle," Judy responded.

Brad looked pensive as he fiddled with the catch rope tied to his saddle horn. "Judy girl, I'm sorry I was an asshole for a while there."

Judy laughed. "What do you mean for a while? Being a well-intentioned asshole is part of your charm."

Brad blushed. He looked hurt.

"Geeze, Brad. I'm just teasing. We got through it."

"You're my sister, you know. In all the ways that matter, you're the best sister a guy could have."

It was Judy's turn to blush, moved by this expression of affection, especially knowing how difficult that was for Brad. "And you're my brother, Brad Kenton, which means I'm duty bound to kick your ass when you get out of line."

"Sounds like a plan to me," Brad responded.

As they neared the house, the cowhands heard a sound as sweet as any worker ever heard. Kathleen was ringing the triangular dinner bell hanging outside the backdoor of the house.

"We having your beans and cornbread?" one of the Bar-D hands asked Judy.

"Feed bag's gotten better around here," Judy responded. "Not sure what Martha and Julie brought, but Kathleen had the makings for chicken enchiladas and sopapillas."

Before leaving to herd the cows back to pasture, Judy and Brad had thrown fresh hay to the bawling calves still contained in the corrals. They would let them all settle for a day or so before putting them through the trauma of branding and castration. Judy was a pragmatic rancher, but it always broke her heart to watch the calves go through this traumatic life event. The calves set up a constant cacophony of noise, mooing and bawling.

As they rode up to the house, Pookie placed her horse next to Judy's.

"Good gosh, they're loud," Pookie said.

"Yep, I highly recommend sleeping with ear plugs the next few nights," Judy responded.

Once in the ranch yard, the cowhands quickly unsaddled their horses, loading them into trailers with Pookie and Judy releasing their horses, including Kathleen's paint, into the horse pasture behind the house. Kathleen and the Kenton women had set up a buffet in the yard by the house, and the hungry cowhands descended on the offering of enchiladas, pot roast with potatoes and carrots, stewed squash and onions, fresh made bread, cucumber and onion refrigerator pickles, a cake, and two kinds of pie. It was a feast fit for a king or any hard working cowhand. A cooler of beer and sodas complimented the pitchers of iced tea and water.

Conversation ceased as soon as the crew had filled the enameled metal plates the Proctors had used for field dinners for over ninety years. The three women in the kitchen crew joined the cowhands, filling their plates amply, having worked just as hard as the dust covered cowhands. For some minutes, the only sounds were the clink of cutlery against plates and the occasional hiss of the opening of a soda or beer. It was a companionable silence.

In distance, a vehicle turned off the highway and down the county dirt road. No one spoke, but all eyes turned to the vehicle, the entire crew waiting to see who approached.

"Oh, Hell," Judy said when the battered gray SUV came close enough to be recognized.

"Fuck," Pookie added. Both Bar-D cowhands started in surprised and then stared wide-eyed at the tiny woman they'd just met.

"Would have been nice if he'd come early enough to help with the work," Joe Bob commented.

"Who is it?" a Bar-D hand asked.

"It's our fire chief, Guy Guyette," Brad said.

The two Bar-D hands looked at each other. "Sounds like you folks aren't real fond of him," one said.

Kathleen sliced at the roast beef on her plate with such vehemence that the knife grated against the enamel. "You might say that," she responded.

Brad turned to the two hands, pausing to think, seeking a quick explanation for the two outsiders. "He damn near got Judy killed."

"What?" one hand said.

"That he did," Joe Bob added.

The other Bar-D hand turned to Pookie. "Well then, I have to agree with you," he said.

"Yeah," the other added. "Fuck."

"Fella' thinks he's shit-on-a-stick when he's really only a fart-on-a-toothpick," Harold said.

"Damn! He must be a piece of work. You folks are some of the nicest and most patient people I've ever known," one Bar-D hand said.

The SUV pulled into the drive and slid to a halt, covering the eating workers in a cloud of dust. Guy stepped from the vehicle. He walked with his head high, chest out, and stomach tucked tight, sauntering toward the group.

"Thought I'd come make sure you weren't creating any fire hazards," he said as he walked.

"It's all fine, Guy. We know what we're doing." Judy looked at the new arrival and fought a brief internal battle between her distaste for the man and her deep-seeded values of country hospitality. "Grab a plate and help yourself," she finally said.

Guy looked surprised and then undecided. Judy watched as his gaze lit on the buffet of fine food. There was hunger in his eyes unlike any Judy had ever seen before. She found herself wondering how often this odd little man ever enjoyed a real, home-cooked meal.

"Eat. There's plenty," Judy said. She ignored the scathing look Kathleen sent her direction.

Guy rushed to the table, filling a heaping plate and taking a beer from the cooler. He found a seat on the ground underneath a shade tree far from the group. All eyes watched as he attacked the food with intense hunger.

Harold looked intently at Judy until he caught her attention. He smiled softly and nodded approval. Judy heard his telepathic message. *You'd make your folks proud*, she felt him think.

It only took a few minutes for the atmosphere of camaraderie to return.

"That sure is a fine hat you got there," a Bar-D hand said to Pookie.

Pookie took her now dusty and sweaty derby from her head and studied it. "It doesn't look as good as it did when I bought it. Judy said I had to have a hat."

"Looks better to me. You got the sweat and dust of a real cowhand," Judy said.

Pookie blushed and smiled, obviously pleased.

"I'll admit you done good today," Harold said.

"Yep, but you're the first cow puncher I ever saw with blue hair," a Bar-D boy said. The grin he gave Pookie was a warning sign to anyone who knew ranching. The teasing had just begun. Judy sat perfectly still, waiting to see how Pookie responded.

Pookie smiled at the cowboy. "At least I don't talk a blue streak, like some people I've met today."

The other Bar-D hand laughed and slapped his companion on the back. "You got yourself a winner here," he said, directing his remarks at Judy.

"She'll do," Judy said.

The sound of Guy's metal plate hitting the ground drew everyone's attention. They watched as he stood, leaving his plate and beer can under the tree.

"Mystifies me why women want to pretend like they're men," he said, walking toward the group.

For a moment, nothing was said, but the atmosphere was charged. One Bar-D hand looked toward Pookie, shook his head, and quietly mouthed the word "fuck."

In the silence, Judy stared at Guy, shaking her head in disbelief. "You're welcome," she finally said.

"For what?" Guy asked.

"For the meal. You know, we're not a restaurant here. You need to take your plate and silverware to the tub by the table and put your beer can in the trash," she said.

Harold chuckled softly and looked toward Judy. "That's my girl," he said.

Guy looked around the group, ignoring Judy's instructions. "Who's the boss here today?" he asked.

"I am," Judy answered.

Guy walked up to her, standing over her. "No matter how hard you try, you're never going to grow a dick," he said.

Judy placed her plate on the ground and stood. Despite the fact that she was four inches shorter than the man and at least seventy pounds lighter, Guy took a step back, a hint of fear in his eyes.

"It's time for you to leave," Judy said.

"Not until I make sure you have a permit to start a fire for any branding you plan to do," Guy said.

The sound of Joe Bob's laugh re-directed attention to him. "We all know that's not required, Guy. You're just being a pain-in-the-ass," he said with forced patience.

By now, everyone was on their feet. Guy looked around, surprised. "I'm the fire chief, and I say what's required," Guy responded.

"Maybe not for long," Harold said.

"You…you need me. You bunch of rookies don't even know how to order equipment or trucks," he said.

"We'll learn," Joe Bob responded.

Guy turned directly to Brad. "What's wrong with you men? You know what I'm talking about, don't you? You're the deputy chief. No woman can do the job. What are you doing taking orders from this bitch?" Guy pointed an accusing finger toward Judy.

It was a right hook, and it was a damn good one. Brad placed it square on Guy's chin, and the unwelcome visitor flew back, lying on the ground, rubbing his chin, stunned.

"Thanks," Judy said to Brad.

"No problem. After all, what's a soul brother for?" Brad responded.

Guy scrambled unsteadily to his feet. "I'll be

calling the sheriff about this," he said.

"Go right ahead. We don't take kindly to invasive trespassers around here," Martha said.

Guy dusted himself off and walked unsteadily to his SUV. As he opened the door, he glared at Judy. Never in her life had she seen such open hatred. As he drove out of the yard, Guy's back tires flung dirt and gravel at the group.

"Damn! He is a piece of work," a Bar-D hand said.

Harold now stood beside the food table, lifting the plastic cover off of the carrot cake his wife had made and noting the plastic wrap over the two pies. "At least he didn't get any dirt in the dessert."

The unwanted visitor was more-or-less forgotten as they all turned their attention to important business...dessert.

Chapter Twenty-one

Surprise

Driving while annoyed makes the miles seem longer. Judy approached the fire station a bit faster than needed. She wanted to get the job done and get back to the ranch. She and Kathleen had already finished the morning rounds checking cattle, including the recently released yearlings who survived the trauma of weaning and branding. None seemed overly traumatized as they adjusted to life without mothers. Good grass, cool water, and warm summer sunshine triggered the natural bovine passion for contentment. Pookie stayed in the workshop, adding to the life-sized metal buffalo sculpture. After she and Kathleen returned from checking cattle, Judy resumed her role as sculptor assistant.

Watching and helping the young artist gave Judy a great sense of pleasure. *Is this what it's like to have a daughter,* Judy wondered. When the phone rang, Judy grudgingly picked up the workshop extension, saving Kathleen the duty of answering the phone. In the house, Kathleen sat at her desk, focused on meeting an article deadline.

"Proctor Ranch," she answered. She pulled off her welding gloves and threw them on the worktable as she listened. "Did you call the station?" she asked. Another pause in which a frown curled her lips and deepened a crease between her eyes. "All right," she said without pleasure. "I'll meet you there."

Pookie turned her attention from the metal buffalo taking shape before her. She stood within the utility trailer where they were building the heavy creature. It was far easier to load the full-sized art one piece at a time rather than as a completed sculpture. Unloading at the community center would be a different matter, one they would deal with when the time came and with a substantial amount of help.

"Who's that?" Pookie asked.

"UPS," Judy answered. "They have a big shipment for the fire station, but they can't get Guy on the phone, and a signature is required."

"Want me to go with you?" Pookie asked.

"No, keep working." Judy gestured toward the buffalo. "He's really coming together."

"You sure?"

"Yeah. I shouldn't be gone for long."

The UPS truck was already parked beside the station when Judy arrived. Judy knew the driver had called from his cell phone while in route. She parked beside him, then walked toward where he sat in his van, the driver's door open.

"How much you got?" Judy asked.

"About ten boxes and some are heavy," he answered.

Must be the wildland tools and personal gear, Judy thought. "Why don't you back up to that first bay, and we'll unload there?"

"Sounds like a plan," the man responded.

It didn't take long. They unloaded all ten boxes, most oblong with two big, square cubes. Judy signed the electronic tablet for the driver, closing the bay door as he drove away. She turned her attention to the boxes stacked against the wall of what served as the company classroom, an open space where the primary personnel door entered the station and adjacent to the small office. She noticed one oblong box had a large red star written in marker on the side, and her curiosity was piqued.

Guy will be pissed if I open it, she thought. That made her smile with pleasure, and she pulled out her pocketknife as she walked toward the box. It only took a second to slice the clear packing tape holding the top closed, pull the flaps open, and see the contents within.

"Combi tools!" Judy called in pleasure. She'd seen them used in training videos and had seen the pictures. From the very first, this unique tool with a shovel head and pick head on a locking swivel, so that it could be used in a multitude of combinations and purposes, had fascinated her.

"This would be awesome for breaking ice on the water troughs in the winter," Judy mumbled to herself as she pulled one from the box, barely noticing the envelope that fell to the floor as she did so. *Bet I could go online and order some for the ranch,* she thought.

Judy played with the tool for several minutes, figuring out the locking mechanism and rotating it from shovel then pick then perpendicular so that both were accessible. In the videos, that configuration had been especially helpful when "scratching line," the technique by which firefighters created a firebreak ahead of the flames, digging a shallow trench down to dirt. When a creeping ground fire reached the trench, it went no further. Despite her pleasure in the new toy, Judy was still anxious to return to the ranch and helping Pookie. She put the tool back in the box and stooped to pick up the envelope that had dropped.

That's odd, she thought. Judy had expected a packing slip. Instead, it was a plain white envelope with "Guy Guyette" written sloppily on the outside. She picked it up, surprised at its thickness … a least a half inch. As she raised it to put it back in the box, a shaft of sunlight from a nearby window fell on the envelope. Through the plain, white paper, Judy clearly saw the face of Benjamin Franklin.

"Shit," Judy said. She stood for several seconds, staring, shocked, at the envelope in her hand. She took a deep breath before testing the flap on the envelope, seeing how securely it was glued shut. One end was loose, and she gently raised the flap, striving to see inside without opening the envelope. Her fears were confirmed. It was a stack of paper currency. Judy speculated they would all bear Benjamin's portrait.

"Son-of-a-bitch," she mumbled as everything became clear to her—why Guy Guyette was so intent on helping start rural fire departments, why he was so well practiced at taking charge.

"He's a crook. He gets paid to make us buy stuff from companies that pay kickbacks," Judy said loudly, knowing no one would hear but needing to express her anger and frustration. She threw the envelope back in the box as if it was something filthy. Her hand shook as she pulled her cell phone from her pocket. Ted Rome's cell number was on her speed dial.

"Rome here," the city fire chief answered.

"Ted, I don't know what the hell to do," Judy said.

There was a pause. "You got my attention. What's wrong?" Ted said.

"We got wildland tools and gear in this morning.

I opened one of the boxes, one with a big red star written on it. There was an envelope inside with Guy's name on it. Ted, it's full of cash."

"God damn son-of-a-bitch," Ted hissed.

"I said the same thing."

"Did you open the envelope?"

"No. Didn't have to. Wasn't even trying to look inside, but the hundred-dollar bill on top shows through the paper. When I saw that, I lifted the flap just a bit, enough to know there's a stack of bills a half-inch thick."

"Anyone with you?" Ted asked.

"Nope." Judy took a deep breath, realizing where he was going. "No witnesses."

There was a pause. Judy envisioned Ted chewing on his mustache, the way he always did when trying to think through a problem.

"Take pictures…the envelope and the labels on the box…the red star too. Can you seal the box back up where it doesn't look like you opened it?"

Judy walked to the supply cabinet, pulled it open, and saw a roll of clear packing tape inside. "I think so," she answered.

"Do it, then get the hell out of there. If he figures out that someone knows, the man could be dangerous."

"That thought had already occurred to me," Judy said.

"I'll call the sheriff and the DA. Oh, and Judy?"

"Yes?"

"I told Joe Bob yesterday, we already got Guy. He falsified the report on that first fire when you and Pookie saved the Johnson place. I've notified the State Fire Marshall's office, and it's likely he'll be banned from firefighting any place in the state, but that doesn't matter now. He won't be fighting any fires from jail. Now get to it and get out of there."

"I'm on it," Judy said. She disconnected the call then used her phone to take pictures of the envelope with Guy's name on it, pulled back the flap as best she could without opening it and got a shot of the stack of bills. Then she replaced the envelope, closed the box and carefully put new packing tape exactly over the tape she'd already cut. Someone would need to look closely to notice the two layers of tape. She replaced the tape in the cabinet, hastily closing the door as she heard the sound of someone activating the combination lock to the personnel door. She walked rapidly away from the cabinet and toward the door, opening it to a surprised Guy Guyette before he had a chance to finish the combination sequence.

"What you doing here?" he demanded.

"UPS called me. They had a delivery, and they couldn't get hold of you," Judy answered.

"Even a fire chief gets to turn the phone off sometimes," he answered defensively. He pushed past Judy, entering the station. His face lit up when he saw the stack of boxes, and then his expression became clouded as he glanced at Judy.

"You didn't open anything, did you?" he asked.

"I started to, but I figured you'd be pissed," she lied. She was surprised that there was no sense of guilt at the lie. *Dad would understand*, she thought.

"Damn right. I don't need you amateurs messing with my inventory," Guy said.

"Whatever, Guy," Judy said with a sigh. She turned to leave the station, closing the door solidly behind her. She stood in the fresh air, taking deep breathes, willing her heart rate to slow down.

Judy walked quickly to her truck and jumped inside, hastily pulling out of the driveway and onto the road to the safety of home.

❧ ❧ ❧ ❧

Guy felt great. He'd run the bitch off. Now she knew who was boss. He turned his attention to the stack of boxes, smiling with anticipation. He pulled a knife from a sheath on his belt and walked straight toward the box with the red star. His old buddy Sam always used the same code to mark the box intended just for him. Guy thought of it as the Cracker Jack box, the one with the prize inside.

A slight motion in his peripheral vision caught Guy's attention, and he turned his head to see the door to the supply cabinet swing open. *Damn bitch didn't close it right,* he thought. That's when he noticed the packing tape. It wasn't where he'd left it.

Chapter Twenty-two

Crisis

Judy's hands quivered as she removed them from the steering wheel. She'd parked her truck in its usual spot beside the workshop, and she could see the flash of the welder from within the dark cavern of the big building. She sat for several minutes, collecting her composure. *I don't think I've ever been this angry in my life*, she thought. The dogs, Somegood and Useless, waited patiently beside the driver door of Judy's truck, their tails wagging and tongues lolling. Judy smiled at the dogs and felt her mood improve drastically. She stepped from the truck, threw a stick for the collie to chase and knelt to ruffle the mutt, Useless', ragged fur, burying her face in the comforting smell of dog.

"Nothing like a four-legged friend to quiet the soul," Judy said to the dog. Somegood returned, stick in mouth, and she dedicated a hand to each dog, providing the pets they begged to receive.

Judy decided she needed to steady her hands as well as her heart and mind before she handled hot metal and the delicate procedure of the welder. Instead of going into the workshop, Judy turned her steps across the yard to the corrals. Dogs were just fine for comfort, but nothing could match the smell and feel of Jackson, the gelding who had been her partner in pasture and pen for eight years. Judy climbed the fence, not bothering to open a gate. Jackson came directly to her, the other horses milling around the big pen. The gelding put his head over her shoulder, and Judy wrapped her arms around his neck. He nickered softly. Judy felt certain horses were magical. Jackson knew she was there for comfort, not for work or a pleasure ride. Judy's hands steadied and the tension in her gut and heart eased. She ran her hands over her beloved horse, taking time to check him closely for anything that needed attention, including lifting each of his feet to check for any wounds or anomalies. After a thorough check of her primary mount, she turned her attention to the other horses – Big Tom, her late father's horse, Kathleen's paint gelding, and Dan, the gentle gelding that was Pookie's mount now. She crossed to the far side of the lot, taking time to check each animal, enjoying the feel and smell of healthy horses. She didn't hear the kitchen door to the house open and close as Kathleen walked across the farm yard toward the horse pen.

Kathleen had watched from the kitchen window. She'd seen Judy with the dogs and the horses. From their years together, Kathleen knew Judy was troubled, recognizing the signs. She left the computer running, the article she was editing half-finished, and walked toward her lover, willing—no, needing to be present for Judy. When she reached the barn, Kathleen paused, watching and waiting, knowing the horses could give Judy what she needed in this moment. Kathleen leaned against the barn, watching, her heart filled with a love so intense it was an ache. She cherished this moment, watching the woman she loved more than anything or anyone. She stayed behind the barn instead of stepping inside the horse pen, blocked from the view of anyone parked down the county road.

Maybe…maybe that little twist of fate would be enough.

Judy finally turned toward Kathleen, feeling the gaze of her lover more than seeing or hearing her presence. Judy's expression gave Kathleen's heart a pleasantly painful twist. It was a moment she may well have remembered all her life even if…even if she hadn't experienced what followed.

As Judy walked, she glanced down at dirt at her feet, spotting an old horseshoe, nails still in the slots, sticking half out of the ground. *So that's where that went*, Judy thought, remembering when Big Tom threw a shoe last winter. She bent to pull it from the ground.

That would be enough, but just barely.

There seemed no pause, between the crack of a distant rifle shot and the searing pain that tore through Judy's back and shoulder. The force of impact slammed her face down into the ground. Despite the pain, she was instantly up, half-running, half-crawling toward the fence and the safe cover of the barn.

"Judy!" Kathleen cried, jumping on the fence rails, starting the climb toward her lover.

"Get back!" Judy yelled.

A second shot rang out, and a bullet caught Judy in the leg, flipping her onto her side. She was close to the fence, and Kathleen dropped to her knees, reaching through the rails and pulling Judy toward her with every ounce of strength she possessed. Judy lay flat, and Kathleen pulled Judy under the bottom rail and behind the barn as a third shot scattered splinters of wood from the barn wall beside them.

"Judy!" Kathleen held her lover close, oblivious to the blood that now soaked her shirt from the long, shallow wound along Judy's back. "What's going on?"

"It's Guy. I caught him. He's taking bribes." Judy's body shook. A sheen of sweat already covered her face. *Fuck! That hurts*, she thought.

"What's going on?" Pookie yelled from the door of the workshop.

"Get in the shop!" Judy tried to yell, but her voice was a weak imitation of what she hoped to achieve.

Kathleen leaned Judy against the barn, stood, and cupped her hands into a megaphone. "Get inside! Close and lock the shop and call the sheriff. Judy's been shot."

"What?" Pookie responded, starting toward her mentors.

"Get in the shop!" Kathleen yelled again, in a voice not to be disobeyed.

Pookie reversed direction, and the two women watched as the girl pushed the power button beside the shop entrance and the huge door began the trip downward. *Keep her safe,* Judy prayed as she watched Pookie disappear behind the relative safety of the metal door.

Kathleen pulled her fire radio from her belt and keyed the talk button. "Calling all Coldwater personnel. This is Coldwater Seven. Coldwater Four has been shot. Repeat, Coldwater Four has been shot. We need the sheriff and an ambulance." She released the key, and she and Judy listened. There was static and an indistinct voice, words totally unrecognizable.

"The bastard turned off the repeater," Judy said.

Kathleen pulled her cell phone from her pocket, looking at the screen, seeing what she feared. "No signal," she said. "We're too far from the signal booster in the house."

Judy looked up at Kathleen. "We're on our own."

"Do you think he'll come after us?" Kathleen

asked.

"Does a bear shit in the woods?" Judy shook her head, fighting off unconsciousness. With the arm on her uninjured side, Judy reached for Kathleen's hand. "Help me up. We've got to get in the barn."

With Judy leaning heavily on Kathleen, they shuffled toward the large wooden doors of the old barn Judy's grandfather had built. When Judy tried to pull open the latch and grasp the door, Kathleen pushed her aside, and Judy leaned against the barn as Kathleen dragged one side of the double barn door open just enough for them to slip inside. Judy walked unsteadily inside, dragging the injured leg. Once they were both inside, Kathleen pulled the door closed. Judy grabbed an ancient pitchfork from where it leaned near the door. With help from Kathleen's steadying hands, she shoved the handle of the fork through the interior handles of the door.

"'Tain't much, but it will have to do," Judy said.

In the relative calm, Kathleen pulled off her t-shirt and pressed it firmly against Judy's back. "You're bleeding."

"Happens when you get shot," Judy responded.

Kathleen punched Judy lightly on the arm "Damn you! This is no time for jokes."

"Cheers me up." Judy tried to look over her shoulder toward her wound. "How bad is it?"

Kathleen lifted the t-shirt bandage and tore away some of Judy's shirt so she could see better. "It's not deep, but you'll need stitches. Now the leg," Kathleen leaned down but hadn't time to take a good look before they heard a pickup, engine reviving hard, as it pulled into the yard. The sound of tires on dirt and gravel was unmistakable as the truck ground to a halt. The two women watched through one of the wide cracks in the old wood boards of the barn. Guy Guyette jumped from his truck, leaving the driver door open. He held a semi-automatic rifle, a powerful scope mounted on top.

"Where are you, bitch?" he yelled, waving the rifle in the air.

They stepped away from the wall, concerned that Guy might see their shapes. Judy glanced down at the dirt floor, noting the drops of blood she'd left behind.

"Damn, he'll see the blood trail," she said.

"What do we do?" Kathleen asked.

"Pookie will have called the sheriff by now. Help is on the way. We just need to hold him off," Judy answered. Judy looked around the barn, spotting a pile of ancient burlap feed sacks. She shuffled toward them.

"What are you doing?"

"We've got to stop the blood trail," Judy said. "Can't hide until we do that."

"Those are filthy," Kathleen said, pointing toward the sacks.

"If I get an infection, we'll deal with that later."

Working rapidly, the two women piled feed sacks on Judy's wounds, using Judy's pocketknife to cut sacks into strips to secure the impromptu bandages. Even as they worked, both women looked around the barn, trying to plan their next step. Kathleen looked toward the rickety ladder to the hayloft.

"Can you make it up that?" she asked.

"I'll have to," Judy answered.

The barn doors rattled, but the pitchfork handle held. "I know you're in there," Guy yelled. "Come out and we'll make this quick and relatively painless."

"Yeah, right," Judy whispered.

Judy went up the ladder faster than she thought possible, almost oblivious to the pain as she used injured muscles and nerves. Kathleen was right behind her. As they worked together to pull up the ladder, they heard the barn doors rattle as Guy threw his weight against them. They had just settled into a layer of loose hay, deep and fresh when the wood of the century-old pitchfork gave way, and the doors swung open. Guy stumbled inside, the rifle still in his hand. He swung the firearm into the ready position, holding with both hands, his finger on the trigger.

"No use hiding, and once you're gone, no one will know what I do."

Judy leaned close to Kathleen, whispering close to her ear. "He doesn't know you're with me." Kathleen nodded agreement.

Judy realized that pulling up the ladder had an additional benefit. Guy hadn't even looked up, not realizing there had been a way for her to reach the loft.

"You women," Guy spat contemptuously. "Always ruining everything, especially you women who think you're men. It's not right. Not natural." Guy looked into each of the three stalls, once used for horses. He looked behind barrels and boxes, decades of stored junk. "Felt good to shoot you, you know. You'd be dead if you hadn't bent over just as I made my first shot."

As they lay still, Judy noticed the second ladder, the one at the back of the loft that went down into the abandoned tack room. Judy clutched Kathleen's wrist, gaining her attention and motioning toward the ladder; she leaned close to whisper again.

"If he realizes we're up here, go for the ladder," she said. "I'll keep him occupied while you sneak around behind him."

Kathleen nodded agreement. She leaned close to whisper back. "Help will be here soon."

Guy continued to circle around the barn. The two women watched as best they could while staying hidden. The man spotted the old door to the tack room, kicking it open and looking inside. Almost immediately, they heard the creak of the ladder.

"Shit!" Judy said. "Plan B."

"What's that?" Kathleen asked.

"Jump."

They did. Kathleen managed to roll easily, using the skills Judy taught her about avoiding injury when thrown from a horse. Injured back, shoulder, and leg handicapped Judy. She landed hard and with such intense pain that her vision darkened, starting from the outside and narrowing to a tunnel of light. Judy fought the darkness with every ounce of consciousness, but she still couldn't make herself move. Kathleen jumped up, grabbing Judy by the shoulders. She started toward the open doors until a wild shot was fired from above. She reversed direction and jumped, pulling Judy with her to a space behind an old water barrel. Judy managed to get enough physical control to push upward and to the side with her legs, helping Kathleen propel them to momentary safety.

Guy jumped too, landing with surprising agility. He stood, facing the two huddled women.

"What do you know? A two for one special." He pointed the rifle toward them, so close he didn't bother to use the scope but just pointed from the hip. "I'm going to enjoy this." He paused, a look of intense pleasure on his face.

Judy felt Kathleen crouch, ready to spring. Judy knew that the second Kathleen moved, she'd be dead, so she held her back, cherishing these few seconds, closing her eyes and progressing to Plan C – praying for a miracle. When she heard the shot, Judy screamed in agony, not from physical pain but because she didn't feel new pain. The bullet hadn't been for her. *Kathleen, no, not Kathleen,* she thought in agony.

Kathleen screamed too. *Judy, no, not Judy,* was her own agonized thought.

In the confusion, an awareness drifted into Judy's consciousness. *Wrong...the sound was wrong,* she thought. The blast had not been from a rifle. Judy realized it had been a shotgun. An airy gurgle caught the attention of both women; they looked up to see Guy on the ground, the rifle beside him. Bubbles of blood, mixed with the air from his lungs, flowed from his mouth and nose, and the front of his shirt was mangled and bloody, a hole the size of a half-dollar in his chest. The gurgling stopped as he exhaled his final breath.

Judy looked toward the barn door opening. Silhouetted against the bright daylight was a tiny woman, a shotgun in her hand.

"Pookie," Judy said.

Pookie walked into the barn, staring at the man on the ground. "I...I told you I wanted to know what to do if I saw a rattlesnake." Her face was pale and her expression frozen in shock.

Kathleen stood and walked to Pookie, putting her arms around the girl. "You did it, sweetie. You killed the biggest snake of all."

All three women cried in anger and pain but mainly relief. That relief was enhanced as they heard the sound of sirens in the distance.

Chapter Twenty-three

Survived

With her good hand, Judy hit the television "off" button on the remote control that was hard-wired into the hospital bed. She was careful not to hit accidentally the nurse call button. She had done so once in the night, when she'd shuffled restlessly, striving to find the position that caused the least discomfort to injured back and leg. The sour-faced night nurse had been so unpleasant about the mishap, that Judy now felt that the nurse call button was best saved for life-threatening needs.

"If you had to get shot, you had a best case scenario," the gray-haired Dr. Cunningham said as he made rounds shortly after Judy's admission. "But we want to keep you a couple of days to watch for signs of infection."

Cunningham had delivered baby Judy. Although he was semi-retired, Judy still preferred his care and she'd asked for him while in the ambulance on her way to the hospital. He was there waiting when she arrived.

"What the hell did you do, Judy Proctor?" the crusty old country doctor asked.

"Guess I'm allergic to bullets, Doc," she answered.

"Then it's best if you stay away from them," he responded.

"I'll keep that in mind, Doc."

In the Emergency Room of the tiny Dulson County Hospital, Judy had received seventeen stitches in the shallow wound in her back. They'd done little more than bandage the entrance and exit wounds to the meaty part of her left thigh. Dr. Cunningham huffed with disapproval when the paramedic showed him the filthy burlap bags they'd used to cover Judy's wounds.

"Why didn't you just lie down and 'waller' in the dirt?" the doctor asked.

"At the time, we were more worried about bullets than dirt," Judy answered.

Dr. Cunningham's face turned an angry red. His face reminded Judy how much this gruff but kindly man cared about his patients.

"Who the hell did this?" Cunningham asked as he probed the exit wound in her leg, assessing the extent of damage. Judy refrained from expressing pain. She realized Cunningham knew her. He was counting on her toughness to expedite his examination.

"Fella' the name of Guy Guyette," Judy answered.

"They catch him?"

"He's dead."

The doctor stopped the examination, shifting his attention to her face. "You kill him?"

"Pookie Thompson did. Young woman who's living with Kathleen and me right now and helping out on the ranch. Saved our lives, she did."

Cunningham nodded his head in approval. "Good for her."

It was the third day of Judy's hospital stay, and she was getting cranky. Most of the staff in the tiny hospital knew and loved the Proctor family, and the story of Judy and Kathleen's near death experience spread across the county quickly. The tale was old news by the time it made it to the pages of the local bi-weekly paper. The semi-private room where Judy stayed was chosen, not to contain two patients, but so that Kathleen could stay watching after her partner in relative comfort. Flowers and potted plants overflowed past the tiny side table between the beds, even the ledge that extended across one wall under the outside window. Flowers had begun to accumulate on the floor.

Judy turned her attention from the now silent television to the two guests who had just taken seats in chairs under the wall-mounted television.

"Sure is sweet of you guys to drive all the way over from Amber just to see me," Judy said to April and Sophie.

"And to relieve me from having to deal with a cranky patient," Kathleen said from where she sat on the room's second bed. The Sapphire novel she'd been reading lay face down on the covers beside her.

"Cranky is a good sign. Means she's ready to get out of here," April said.

Sophia laughed a soft throaty laugh. "I agree, and I hope you don't mind that we came for more than just a hospital visit." She lifted her leather briefcase from the floor and put it on her knees.

Judy sat up stiffly, moving awkwardly because of her injuries. "What's up?"

"We've been doing a little digging about this Guy Guyette fellow," April said.

Sophia pulled a stack of papers from her briefcase. "The social security number he gave your fire department was fraudulent, but he wasn't very smart."

"How's that?" Kathleen asked.

"It belongs to a Georgia woman who died fifteen

years ago."

"What the heck?" Judy said. "Why'd he use that number?"

"That's where he wasn't smart," April said. "The woman's name was Bertha Pendergrass."

Sophie dug through the papers, finding a photocopy of a newspaper article. She stood and handed it to Kathleen. "When we looked up her obituary, there wasn't much, barely a paragraph, but it did say she had one surviving son."

Kathleen looked at the article and then gave a humorless laugh. "Guyette Pendergrass of South Bend, Georgia," she read.

"Well crap," Judy said. "Was he even a firefighter?"

"That he was, and a good one, it seems. He was captain of the South Bend Fire Department, until—" April said.

Sophia interrupted. "Until he was charged with assault and attempted rape of a female member of his company. Charges are still pending. That's one reason we came to Dulson in person. We need to take documentation to the sheriff's office. They should send a DNA sample from Guy to the South Bend authorities. That's the only way we can legally prove that Guy Guyette is really Guy Pendergrass."

"When did this happen?" Judy asked.

Sophie riffled through the papers again, pulling out a legal document. She studied the paper, looking for a date. "Charges were filed October twentieth two years ago."

"Damn! The girl okay?" Judy asked.

"What girl?" Sophia asked.

"The one he attacked."

"The articles don't say. My guess is she'll be glad

to hear the news of what happened to him," April said.

"Pookie needs to know," Kathleen said.

There was a silence in the room.

"How's she taking it?" April asked.

From the bedside tray table, Judy grabbed a magazine and thwacked it angrily against the bed. "Some ways I'm madder at Guy for what he did to her than to me. I can't imagine what it's like to kill someone, even a snake like him."

"I'll be okay," a voice said from the doorway.

They all turned to see Pookie standing there, Ted Rome in the hallway behind her. The two walked inside. Kathleen jumped off the bed and gave Pookie a welcoming hug.

"You up to a little more company?" Ted asked Judy.

"Better than sitting here watching soap operas or rerun Westerns," Judy answered.

Ted turned to April and Sophia, shaking their hands as Judy made introductions. "I heard some of what you were telling Judy and Kathleen about Guyette. Pookie and I have more to add."

"What?" April asked.

"State police have taken over investigating the cash Judy found with the wildland tools. When they went to the salesman Guy bought the equipment from, he squealed liked a greased pig. Long story short, turns out Guy has a long habit of taking kickbacks from vendors. Police searched his house and found nearly a quarter million dollars in cash."

"That explains how he's been able to avoid detection. He had plenty of money to pay for forged identity documents," Sophia said.

"And fire qualifications. The documents he

showed us looked real," Kathleen added.

"He'd been a firefighter for over twenty-five years. He probably had authentic ones for forgers to use as templates," Sophia said.

Pookie was uncharacteristically quiet. Judy ceased paying attention to the overall conversation and was focused on her young mentee. "Come here, kiddo." Judy motioned for Pookie to sit on the edge of the bed. "Are you sure you're okay?"

Pookie leaned back, careful to avoid Judy's injured leg, and looked at the ceiling. "I...I've had some bad dreams, but...but I'm really glad you and Kathleen are okay."

Judy squeezed Pookie's arm lovingly. "We owe you our lives."

Pookie looked at Judy, tears in her eyes. "You don't owe me anything! We're family. I just did what I had to do. He shouldn't...he shouldn't have hurt my moms." Kathleen crossed the short distance between the beds, and the three women merged into a spontaneous group hug.

An empty room could not have been any more silent. The silence was broken as Ted shuffled his feet uncomfortably. "I guess...I guess knowing you ladies has made me look at what family means a little differently." Ted cleared his throat. "Pookie and me, we got some more news."

Pookie pulled away from the group hug and smiled shyly, the first smile Judy had seen on Pookie's face since before the shooting. "Yeah, good news."

"What?" Judy asked.

"I've decided what I'm going to do about, you know, education...a job," Pookie said.

"Terry will be eager to hear this," April said.

"I already called her," Pookie said.

Ted stood tall and proud. "Think you can do without your top hand for a few weeks, Judy?"

"For a good reason I can," Judy responded.

"You folks out at Coldwater have done so well with your rural station that I've got a couple more of the rural communities that want to start a station. I've convinced the county commissioners that I can't oversee it all by myself. They've authorized me to hire a part-time county coordinator." He crossed the room and patted Pookie on the shoulder. "I've offered the job to this little firebrand here, but she'll have to go to the state fire academy first."

The women converged on Pookie, rounds of congratulations filling the air.

Dr. Cunningham stood in the doorway. "What the hell's going on here? This is a hospital, not a social club."

"Well heck, Doc. That's what you get for keeping a healthy woman cooped up for so long," Judy responded.

"Guess you better just go home then," he responded.

"Works for me," Judy responded.

"I'll give the nurse your release order and some prescriptions. I don't ever again want to see you with any bullet holes. Hear me?"

"Yes, sir," Judy answered.

The doctor turned and strode away. Judy's feet were over the edge of the bed before he was out of the doorway.

"Where's my clothes?" she demanded.

Kathleen turned to the group of visitors. "Thanks for coming, but unless you want to watch Judy do a striptease, it's probably time to go."

"I'm outta here," Ted said, as he headed for the door.

"He's my ride," Pookie said, following him out the door.

Sophia stood gracefully and then stared down at her lover. April sat unmoving.

"Ready?" Sophia asked her.

"To leave or enjoy the show?" April answered.

"*Madre de dios!*" Sophia grabbed April by the hand and pulled her to her feet. She turned to look at Kathleen. "What am I going to do with her?"

At this point, Judy was limping toward the small closet where Kathleen had stashed a suitcase. "Did you bring me clothes? They cut off the ones I was wearing when they brought me in."

Kathleen looked at Sophia. "Don't ask me. I can't figure out how to handle the one I've got."

Epilogue

Happy Endings

Pookie was resplendent in her new dress firefighter uniform, her brass badge polished to a mirror-like sheen. She scanned the crowd of people milling in the yard of the Coldwater Community Building and Fire Station. Pookie thought she'd met everyone in the area, but she had no clue who half of them were.

"Damn!" Pookie overheard old Mr. Johnson say as he stood beside the life-sized metal buffalo. "Never thought Coldwater would have its own sculpture park."

His wife looked on, shaking her head. "Oh hush! Just enjoy. Besides being real art, the women who made it were the ones who saved our place from burning to the ground. Something they wouldn't have needed to do if you had just…"

"Leave me be, woman. I won't dump the trash burn barrel in the arroyo ever again."

Pookie laughed quietly as Judy and Kathleen stepped to her side. In the months since the shooting, Judy had progressed from crutches to cane and finally to a slight limp. Through it all, she'd never stopped working, although she had grudgingly allowed Pookie and Kathleen to do more around the ranch than before.

"So how does it feel to be the featured artist at your very own opening reception?" Judy asked.

"It was both of us," Pookie responded.

"You designed it. You built it. I was just the helper," Judy said.

"However it was done, I'm proud of both of you," Kathleen said. She stepped between the two, placing an arm around each of their shoulders. Kathleen turned her attention to the sculptures themselves, now resting in their permanent home. Pookie, Judy, and their crew of volunteer helpers, mainly other firefighters, had finished placing the heavy sculptures earlier that week.

The massive buffalo led the way. The structure was built entirely of bits of scrap metal, but somehow managed the effect of a living, breathing king of the plains. In a trail behind him, piles of stylized buffalo droppings were colorfully coated in polished enamel, starting with brown and green in the chips themselves, but surrounded with metal undulating fingers in red, yellow and orange, depicting the fire fuel the chips provided, making settlement of the plains possible. A smaller but still impressive Longhorn steer followed the buffalo, trailed by his own fiery droppings. A Hereford heifer, also in stylized scrap metal, finished the trio, but the cow-pies took on a different theme behind her. Instead of fire, growing from the droppings were metal depictions of wheat, sorghum, and corn, finishing the artistic depiction of the evolution of agriculture on the High Plains.

Curley Thomas approached the three women, a half-eaten homemade donut in his hand and crumbs on his shirt front.

"I like these art opening shindigs. Did you see the spread of food laid out in the community center? Makes our Coldwater holiday dinner look like a snack bar," Curley said.

"Who are all these people?" Pookie asked.

Judy looked around at the crowd. "Folks from all over the county. Nobody's going to miss dedication of the first sculpture in Dulson County."

"There's never been another sculpture?" Pookie asked.

"When I was a kid, they had a statue of a World War I soldier on the courthouse lawn, but that was on loan from Texas Tech. They took it back when I was in high school," Curley said.

"I didn't know that," Judy said.

"No disrespect to veterans, but we were kinda glad to see it go. The artist wasn't very good. Statue looked a little more like a dogcatcher than a soldier." Curley turned to look at Pookie's sculpture. "Now this," he said. "This is for durned tooting a buffalo."

Pookie blushed with pride. Words of praise about art from Curley Thompson meant more to her than accolades from any art critic.

"Thanks, Curley."

"Hey, look there," Judy said, pointing toward the highway and an SUV driving their direction.

"Who's that?" Curley asked.

"Friends of ours from Amber," Kathleen answered.

"You go say 'howdy.'" Curley turned toward the old school house/community center. "I think I'll see what kind of pies they have cut now."

The three women walked toward the road, and Judy waved April toward a space where she could park among the plethora of vehicles already present. Terry opened the door and stepped out of the back seat as soon as the vehicle stopped. She stood before Pookie, studying her from head-to-toe.

"You look—" She glanced to see who was nearby.

"particularly sexy in that uniform."

Pookie leaned close, whispering just to Terry. "I'll look better out of it a little later."

Terry blushed and laughed as she hugged Pookie. "Will you keep the hat on?" she whispered.

It was Pookie's turn to blush.

The other four women stood watching the younger couple.

"I don't know what they're saying to each other, but it looks interesting," April said.

"Oh heck, we don't need to know the details to know the essence," Judy said.

Sophia laughed her throaty laugh. "*Amor juvenil,*" she said.

"What?" Judy asked.

"Young love," Kathleen answered.

April pulled a camera from a bag around her shoulder and walked toward the sculptures. "Wow! Nice work." She snapped pictures of the art and the crowd. "Can I get a shot of you with the buffalo?" she asked Pookie.

"Only if Judy's in it too. She helped build it and taught me how to weld so I could do it."

"I just helped some. Pookie's the artist here."

April scribbled a note on a pad. "Both of you then. Helpers count." Pookie and Judy took positions beside the head of the buffalo.

"This is an amazing crowd," Sophia said.

"Dulson County's first sculpture park. It's a big deal," Kathleen said.

"We're all really proud of Pookie," Judy said.

"Me included," Terry said.

Pookie walked to her lover and squeezed her hand. "That means a lot to me," she said.

"I've got some news too," Terry said.

"She most certainly does," Sophia added.

"You mean besides graduating summa cum laude?" Kathleen said.

"I've been offered three different teaching jobs," Terry said.

Pookie went pale. There was a strain to her smile. "That's...that's awesome. Where?"

"One is in the Dallas school system...another in Colorado Springs," Terry said. She paused, staying silent, a shy smile on her face.

"And, the third is..." April encouraged.

"Oh yeah, the third." Terry smiled with a mischievous twinkle in her eye. "The high school history teacher position at Dulson Independent School District."

"What?" Pookie said.

Terry laughed, grabbed Pookie's hands, and twirled her around. "I've already accepted the job. I start in August."

Pookie forgot the dignity of her uniform and performed a jig. "Yes!"

"Yeah, we thought we might help her look for an apartment this afternoon...or something," April said, glancing toward Judy.

Judy and Kathleen exchanged eye contact, a wordless conversation conducted with raised eyebrows and head tilts.

"Well, seems to me you already have a place," Judy said.

Pookie froze mid-jig. She held her breath, looking back and forth between Terry and Judy.

Terry looked at her feet. "Well, I was rather hoping..."

"It would be a commute," Kathleen said.

"I'll be able to afford a car now," Terry responded.

Brad appeared in the middle of the group of women. "What you bunch of ladies doing? If you don't get inside soon, all my mom's red velvet cake will be gone along with Joe Bob's homemade butternut ice cream."

Judy laughed. "That's settled then."

"What? That it's time to eat?" Brad asked.

"That too," Kathleen responded.

The group herded into the community center, where Pookie was given a hero's welcome and Terry learned just how very welcome she would be in the Coldwater community.

Sometimes life just can't get any better.

About theAuthor

Kayt C. Peck lived the ranch life as a child and young adult and knows the smell, feel, hardships, and gratifications of life on the range. The hard work and determination needed to survive on a Texas farm and ranch helped her as she began a life-long career as a writer that has included working as a journalist, a public-affairs officer in the U.S. Naval Reserve, and as a grants expert writing applications raising over $30 million for worthy domestic and even international organizations. She has published four other novels, one biography, and written a number of plays, including being a two-time awardee in the Rocky Mountain Voices play competition and receiving a special award for Excellence in Play Writing at the American Association of Community Theatres Region VI 2015 finals. She has authored and published numerous articles, short stories, and poems. Her novels *Kiva and the Mosque* and *Good Water* were both finalists in the New Mexico/Arizona Book Awards. Today, she lives quietly in her cabin home in the mountains of northeastern New Mexico.

Other books by Kayt Peck

Good Water- ISBN- 978-1-939062-87-1

The dry plains drew Judy Proctor like a bear to her den…or a moth to the flame. Ranching was her life. The sweat as she branded or "doctored" cattle…the howl of a coyote in the quiet, night air…half-frozen fingers as she cut the wire to loosen hay bales for hungry cattle scratching for survival in snow-covered land…all of the everyday existence on the ranch was her life.
It was where she belonged.
It was a lonely life.

She had tried to leave the ranch to join the "normal" existence of a talented young woman in the city, but it had never been home. When her parents were killed in an automobile accident, she returned to the family ranch as much because she needed it as it needed her. She faced a lonely life to be shared with no better company than Somegood and Useless, her cow dog and the mottled mutt that were her companions.

Kathleen Romero slipped into Judy's life unexpectedly. She came to the plains to write a story. Would she stay because of the real truth she found in the simple drama of husbanding land and animals?

Unfortunately, even wide-open spaces can be plagued by prejudice and closed-minds. As the two women struggle to know each other, they must also carve a place for themselves among the country-folk who have been Judy's friends and neighbors her entire life.

The Ladies Room - ISBN - 978-1-943353-09-3

A dream is housed in the dusty, unused storage room above the Pink Triangle, one of Amber, Texas' two gay bars. Journalist April Sims serves as the reluctant leader in making that dream a reality. Under her guidance an electic group of women build a safe place in a community where being a lesbian can be dangerous and difficult.

April meets Sophia Mendez, a local attorney, as she seeks legal guidance for members of the group. In meeting with the women of the Ladies' Room, Sophia finds herself dealing with personal as well as professional issues.

When a radical religious group levels an attack on the entire gay community, even to the the point of a vigilante attack on the Pink Triangle, the strength and unity of the women of The Ladies' Room will be tested to the core.

Only time will tell if the beauty of the dream can override the ugliness of a harsh reality.

Other titles from Sapphire Books Publishing

The House at the End of the Street – ISBN – 978-1-943353-39-2

Natalie Hargrove, a previously accomplished artist, and Caitlin Cassidy should never have met. After all, Caitlin was only a twelve-year-old girl when Natalie was already dead and gone. But they did meet, and it was that dramatic encounter in the house at the end of the street that changed their lives forever. The moment was so powerful, so important, that it drew Caitlin, now a renowned novelist, back to her hometown twenty years later to seek out Natalie's ghost. Taking up refuge in the dark, broken house, Caitlin believes that getting back to her roots and to the bottom of her experience with the ghost will somehow help heal the wounds her life has brought her.

Against the backdrop of a Victorian mansion, a story unlike any other unfolds between Caitlin and Natalie, and leaves them with one lingering question: even if love is enough to bridge the gap between life and death, is it enough to keep a ghost from passing on?

Unspoken – ISBN – 978-1-943353-35-4

Desiree Chevalier is determined to control her own destiny, and that includes shaking her mother's iron grip on her life. Rosalie Chevalier is not going down without a fight. She's a corporate raider after all and it just wouldn't do to have a wayward daughter. When Desiree steps away from the Chevalier fortune to put herself through Mount Holyoke College, Rosalie decides to show up on her doorstep. Although her mother digs in, Desiree refuses to bend.

Rowan Knight is working just as hard as Desiree to put herself through school. She is intrigued by Desiree but also wary of the icy reception she receives each time they meet. Rosalie's persistent interference in Desiree's life intensifies the tension between Desiree and Rowan. Will they be able to move past the obstacles in their path, or will their love remain unspoken?

The Flaw in Logic – ISBN – 978-1-943353-41-7

This romantic adventure follows Commander R'cey Hawke, bounty hunter. She leads a mission to a backwater world to retrieve one of the Amalgam's most wanted. When her space vessel crash lands, R'cey must work with a group of locals who believe in magic, of all things. R'cey soon finds herself on an epic quest that takes her across unbelievable realms. Battles with harpies, imps, golems, and the Demon Aamon, open her eyes to possibilities other than her own version of reality.

Princess Thalia Dumont's pact with an assassin has an unexpected result. That ill-conceived bargain forces her on a dangerous journey. King Lotar lies under a dark spell and Thalia must find the cure. Along the way, she meets an off-world stranger who will change how she sees the universe.